SHOWTIME

SHOWTIME

Jean Ure

HarperCollins *Children's Books*

First published in Great Britain by
HarperCollins *Children's Books* in 2018
HarperCollins *Children's Books* is a division of HarperCollins*Publishers* Ltd,
HarperCollins Publishers
1 London Bridge Street
London SE1 9GF

The HarperCollins website address is:
www.harpercollins.co.uk

1

Text copyright © Jean Ure 2018
All rights reserved.

ISBN 978-0-00-816454-6

Jean Ure asserts the moral right to be identified as the author of the work.

Typeset in Gill Sans 12/20pt by Palimpsest Book Production Ltd,
Falkirk, Stirlingshire

Printed and bound in England by CPI Group (UK) Ltd, Croydon, CR0 4YY

MIX
Paper from
responsible sources
FSC
www.fsc.org **FSC™ C007454**

Chapter One

"I simply cannot *believe* –" Chloe opened her tote bag and took out a little hammer. Then she picked up one of her pointe shoes – brand-new, sparkly-clean pointe shoes – and began bashing at it. "I simply cannot believe we're in our second year!"

Somewhat soberly I said, "I can't believe we've all survived."

It still made cold, damp goosefeet go plapping down my spine when I thought how close I'd come to being thrown out. At the end of our very first term, that had been. Not because my dancing wasn't up to standard but because Ms Hickman, Head of Ballet, hadn't thought I was committed enough. It was only thanks to Caitlyn that I'd been given a second chance. She had actually been brave enough to speak up for me! What was more, Ms Hickman had actually listened. Which was why I was still here, a year later, on the first day of the new term – sitting in the Green Room next to Studio One, waiting for the studio to clear so that afternoon class could begin. We were all here, all eight of us. Me and Caitlyn, Alex and Roz, Tiffany, Amber, Chloe, Mei. Survivors!

Alex nodded, complacently. "It's practically unheard of, everyone being kept on."

I agreed. City Ballet School has a reputation for being ruthless when it comes to what Mum calls "weeding out". *Too tall, wrong shape, hasn't lived up to earlier promise.*

"We're obviously an exceptionally talented group," I said.

"Oh, Maddy, don't," begged Caitlyn. "Please! It's like tempting fate!"

Personally I felt I'd already tempted fate. Going ice skating and injuring myself halfway through my very first term really had been asking for trouble. Even Sean had lectured me about it, and Sean isn't at all a lecturing kind of person even though he's my big brother and doesn't always take me seriously. Mum and Dad, thank goodness, had never known. I still had nightmares, wondering what Mum would have had to say. She'd said enough when Jen (my sister) had got married and had Thomas and immediately stopped dancing. You'd have thought the world had come to an end! But at least Jen had had an excuse, and now that he was a toddler even Mum thought Thomas was pretty cute. I wouldn't have had any excuse at all. Just as well it had stayed a guilty secret!

I slowly sank down on to the floor, leaning back against the wall, legs comfortably lolling. In just a few minutes I'd be working hard enough, bending, stretching, leaping. Mr Leonardo, who takes us for Character (the class we were waiting for and one of the ones I like best) is a very sweet and lovely man who almost never loses his temper or makes sarcastic remarks (unlike Ms Hickman, who makes them all the time). Mr Leonardo would far sooner praise you for your good points than shame you in front of the whole class by sarcastically informing you that you looked like a sack of potatoes or moved with about as much animation as a slug. For all that, he doesn't believe in letting us relax. Character is a whirl of activity from the word go.

I gazed around, contentedly, at the others. Caitlyn, next to me, was taking the opportunity to finish darning a pair of pointe shoes. Darning pointe shoes is a job I particularly dislike, but Caitlyn actually takes pride in it. She is always so industrious! Chloe, meanwhile, was still merrily bashing with her hammer.

"It always seems such a pity," said Caitlyn, "that we have to do these horrible things." She held up the shoe she'd been working on. Her stitches (unlike mine) are always so neat and precise; she turns darning into some kind of art form. "Honestly," she said, "it makes me feel like a vandal. Those poor shoemakers! It must be absolutely heartbreaking for them... They give us these beautiful, delicate shoes and the first thing we do is destroy them!"

"Yes, and if we didn't," pointed out Tiffany, in her usual crushing tones, "we wouldn't be able to dance in them and there wouldn't be much point in anyone bothering to make them in the first place."

Tiffany is one of those people that has no soul. When I stop to think about it, it does seem rather cruel, the way we treat our shoes. We snip off bits of the satin, we glue and we darn and we batter and bash. Sometimes we even cut the backs to make them fit properly. What Chloe was doing was breaking the shank and softening the block so that her shoes wouldn't make loud clopping noises as she danced. We all do it; you have to. Imagine a whole corps de ballet clip-clopping about like carthorses! And if we didn't darn the toes we wouldn't have a good grip when we went on pointe and would most likely end up on our backs with our legs in the air. But even then, after all our hard work, one pair of shoes would hardly last a full performance. Certainly not in a long ballet like *Swan Lake* or *Giselle*. Not that any of us had reached that stage yet. When we did – if we did, fingers tightly crossed – it would mean having several pairs of shoes all prepared and ready to go, and *that* would mean forever having to darn and hammer and sew on ribbons. As I once bitterly remarked to Sean, it was so much easier for him. Of course he just laughed. This is what I mean about not always taking me seriously.

"If you want to know," said Chloe, pausing for a moment in her labours, "I'm not just bashing my shoes, I'm bashing *somebody*."

Amber said, "Ooh! Who?"

"Just somebody," said Chloe. "Actually, if you really want to know, a boy."

"*Oh?*"

That got everyone's attention, including mine. Heads shot up all over the room.

"Tell, tell!" said Tiffany. "What boy?"

"Boy called Dominic."

"So who is he and why are you bashing him?"

"Cos he's an idiot! I've known him, like, forever. Our mums are best friends and him and me were at primary school together."

"And you're bashing him because…?"

"Cos, like I said, he's an idiot! I bumped into him yesterday and he told me –" Chloe bashed with renewed vigour – "he actually *told* me, he was very sorry but he just didn't get it with ballet… he said he found it boring."

"Has he ever actually seen any?" said Roz.

"Yes. He tried watching *Fille mal* on television."

"He doesn't even like *Fille mal*?" Caitlyn's voice rose to a high-pitched squeak of disbelief. "It's one of my favourite ballets!"

"It's everyone's favourite ballet," I said. "Well, after *Swan Lake* and *Giselle*. And maybe *Nutcracker*." How could it not be? It's so happy and funny and romantic, all at the same time. You'd have to have a heart of stone not to enjoy *Fille mal gardée*. Or, maybe, just be a boy.

 7 ☆

Caitlyn might squeak, but on the whole, it has to be said, most boys aren't into ballet.

"What about the Clog Dance?" said Roz.

Amber said, "Yes! What about the Clog Dance?"

Someone started humming the music, which had me on my feet in an instant. (To be honest, I don't need much encouragement!) Chloe immediately joined me. Together, we clog-danced happily across the floor. The ballet is so familiar that we pretty well know it step by step, though in fact the Clog Dance is actually danced by a man dressed up as a woman (the Widow Simone). It's one of the funniest things in ballet, I think.

"I just don't see," said Alex, "how *anyone* can say they don't love the Clog Dance!"

To be fair, Chloe said, he hadn't minded that bit so much. "He thought it was like pantomime."

There was a moment of silence while we wondered whether or not we should be offended. Then Caitlyn gave a sigh and said, "I suppose he's right, in a way. It's not my most favourite part."

Kindly I said, "No, cos you like the romantic bits."

She was happy to admit it. "I love the romantic bits! I think they're really touching."

"*He* doesn't," said Chloe. "He says for him it's all too pink and pretty."

Loud groans filled the room. Eyes rolled.

Apologetically Chloe said, "He's actually quite nice. He only tried watching cos he wanted to be able to talk to me about it."

Tiffany tossed her head. "Just a pity he couldn't find anything sensible to say!"

I don't very often agree with Tiffany, but on this occasion I did. I don't mind people not liking ballet; I don't like lots of things. Opera, for instance, and golf. How my dad can sit for hours watching golf on television I really don't know. Boring, boring, boring! So I reckon it's OK if some people are bored by ballet. But *pink and pretty*… that is so insulting!

It was just as well, I thought, that the boys weren't yet here. It would have made some of them really angry. Josh and Carlo for sure. It didn't take much to get them going! Finn and Oliver, and maybe Kanye, might have just shrugged it off. They're not as hot-headed as the other two. I was really glad that Nico hadn't heard, though. Nico was my partner – for *pas de deux*, that is. Not all of the time, cos they like to switch us about a bit, but mostly we danced together. It had made us quite close; we often confided in each other. I knew, for instance, that Nico had had to fight really hard to become a dancer. Not only had his dad been dead set against the idea but he'd also been bullied quite badly at school because of it. He'd once told me that I didn't know how lucky I was, coming from a ballet family.

It's true that I've lived and breathed ballet for just about as long as I can remember. Mum and Dad both used to dance with City Ballet, Mum being specially famous for her *Firebird* and Princess Aurora in *Sleeping Beauty*, Dad being more of a character dancer. Dad has always been more interested in choreography than in actual dancing, which is why he now flies all over the world, to America, Australia, and even once to Russia, to put on his ballets. Mum, meanwhile, runs her own ballet school, which she rules with a rod of iron, almost worse even than Ms Hickman. I know, cos she was the one that trained me! She trained Jen and Sean too. If Jen hadn't given up her career to be a full-time mum, she'd still be with the company today. Sean, of course, still is.

When I come to think about it, Sean has really had it easy. Certainly compared with Nico. I'm sure nobody has ever given Sean a hard time. I'd like to see them try!

The boys, by now, were starting to arrive.

"What are we waiting for?" said Josh. "Is someone still in there?"

I explained that it was members of the company. The Millennium Hall, where City Ballet performs, is only a few minutes away from the school – just a short walk down the Cut, near Waterloo station – so if they run out of rehearsal space they tend to come and use one of our studios, instead.

"It's about time they were out! What are they rehearsing, anyway?"

I shook my head. "I don't know."

"Let's go take a look."

We clustered outside the studio door, gazing through the glass panel. I could see Sean and Sergei Ivanov, another of the company's leading dancers. They were moving energetically about the studio, ducking and dodging and every now and again lunging at each other. I couldn't hear any music but I knew at once what they were doing.

"It's *Romeo and Juliet*," I said. The death of Mercutio. Very dramatic! "I'd forgotten they were bringing that back. It hasn't been in the repertoire for ages."

The others jostled to get a better look.

"Who's dancing what?"

"Sean's Mercutio, Sergei's Tybalt."

"I hate Tybalt," said Caitlyn. "I can't ever forgive him

for killing Mercutio. Mercutio is so fun! Tybalt's just a bully."

"Well, but Mercutio does provoke him," said Roz. "He does show off, rather."

"That's no excuse!" cried Caitlyn. And "Oh!" she wailed, turning her head away.

Oliver waved a hand. "Bye-bye, Mercutio!"

We all watched as Tybalt's sword (imaginary, for rehearsal purposes) found its mark, plunging deep into Mercutio's back.

"How cowardly is *that*?" said Caitlyn.

"Only way he could get him," said Oliver.

We watched as Mercutio went staggering off, reeling and swaying, trying bravely to make out that he was all right, but growing steadily weaker until, in the end, his strength gave way and he sank down, mortally wounded.

Caitlyn wailed, "Oh, I hate this scene! When I first saw it, I really didn't think he was going to die. Now I just can't bear to watch it!"

"It's one of the best bits," said Carlo.

"It's not! It's heartbreaking."

"But I thought *Romeo and Juliet* was one of your favourite ballets?" I said.

"They're all her favourites." Tiffany said it scathingly. "Just name me one ballet you don't positively adore."

"There are lots I don't adore!"

"So, go on… tell me one."

Roz cackled. "Anything that Sean's not in!"

Caitlyn's cheeks immediately turned pink. She is so easy to tease!

"I don't much like *ZigZag*," she said. "He dances in that."

And then she glanced at me, obviously worried I might think she was being disrespectful. *ZigZag* is one of Dad's ballets, but it's a very early one from what Mum calls his abstract period. No storylines, just pure dance. It's known in the family as Dad's bendy ballet, cos of all the weird shapes the dancers have to twist themselves into.

"You're just a hopeless romantic," I told Caitlyn. "I

bet you wouldn't mind half so much if it was Sergei that got killed!"

The fact is she has this massive crush on my brother, though to be fair she's not alone in that. I should think half the little ballet fans in the country have photos of Sean stuck on their bedroom walls. It really was time she started to grow out of it, though.

"Speaking personally," said Tiffany, "I adore *ZigZag*. I think it's really inventive."

"It hasn't got a lot of soul," I said.

"So what? It's clever! Makes a nice change from peasants doing their jolly peasant dances. You can get a bit sick of that."

I privately agreed with her, but I wasn't about to say so. It doesn't do to agree too much with Tiffany. It just puffs her up and makes her even more big-headed than she already is.

"I don't actually think that *ZigZag* is one of Dad's best," I said, "but I can see it might be your sort of thing."

Tiffany bristled, immediately suspicious. "What's that supposed to mean, *my sort of thing*?"

"Well…" I waved a hand. All I'd meant was that it suited her style of dancing: very brittle and showy without much in the way of emotion. Still, I didn't want it to seem like I was criticising her; not on our first day back. We were bound to rub each other up the wrong way sooner or later – we always did. But for the moment I was in too good a mood to say anything that might upset her, even if she did tend to get on my nerves.

"It's a ballet that needs a really strong technique," I said. "That's all."

Tiffany made a little grunting sound.

"Not everybody could manage it," I said.

"You could," said Caitlyn. "You've got a strong technique."

I said, "Yes, but technique's not everything. I prefer parts where I can act as well as dance."

"Obviously runs in the family," said Oliver. He staggered and clutched at himself. "That was some death scene!"

Caitlyn pushed at him. "Stop it!"

"Why?" Oliver grinned. "It's a great piece of acting!"

"I wish he'd dance Romeo," said Caitlyn. "Why does he have to dance Mercutio? I'm sure he could dance Romeo, if he wanted."

"Well, but Romeo dies too," I said.

"Only right at the end. At least I could enjoy it up till then."

"Oh, you're such a softie!" jeered Roz.

Caitlyn hung her head. "I can't help it. I don't like sad things."

"*Giselle*'s sad," I said. "You adore *Giselle*!"

Roz cackled and said, "That's cos it's only Giselle that dies and not Sea— Oops!" She clapped a hand to her mouth. "Sorry! I mean Albrecht."

We stood back as Sean and Sergei left the studio. There was a time when I might have said something, even if it was just "Hi". To Sean, I mean. Everyone knows he's my brother, but some people – Tiffany, for instance, and Amber, who's her best friend – seemed to think it was gross for a lowly dance student to address one of the company's big stars without being invited, so I'd trained myself to be discreet and make like we were nothing to do with each other. *I* couldn't help it if he winked at me as he came through the door. Or maybe it was at Caitlyn. She obviously thought it was, the way her cheeks slowly turned from blushing pink to bright red. I made a mental note to tell him he really must stop teasing her like that. How was she supposed to get over him if he kept encouraging her?

Mr Leonardo had obviously arrived early as he was there waiting for us.

"Well, that, of course, was *Romeo and Juliet*," he said. "A brand-new production. You'll no doubt be learning some of the dances this term so I would urge you all to go and see it as soon as you can. Now, just briefly, before we begin, I have a bit of news. You all know, of course, that at the end of term we have the big summer show where you'll be put through your paces —"

Showtime! The most important event of the year – the one we were all working towards. How you performed then could determine the whole of your future.

"Just put it on the back burner for the moment," said Mr Leonardo, "because in the meantime we have another event lined up. A rather exciting one. As I'm sure you're aware, CBS is part of the Ballet Outreach programme, taking ballet into the community. Last term, some of you may remember, a group of our senior students went into one of the local schools, Cardinal Fisher, which went down so well that the school has now asked whether it would be possible for a few of their Year Eight pupils, the ones who expressed the most appreciation – which I'm happy to say included boys as well as girls – to actually visit us here. So! I think you'll agree that's excellent news. We've arranged that a small group, about twenty in all, will be coming to us later in the term, and your year have been chosen to be their hosts! Which, I may say, is a great honour. You will, in effect, be ambassadors for the ballet."

He paused, to let that sink in. We preened ourselves. Ambassadors!

"So here's the plan. I thought that to kick off we'd show them what a normal class is like – well, a sample of a normal class. Obviously not a full class, there wouldn't be time. Let's say about half an hour, and then I propose we demonstrate how we put our technique into practice. Mrs Elkins and I have sat down with Ms Hickman and we've come up with a list, which I have here –" he waved a sheet of paper at us – "of what you'll all be dancing. They'll only be very short pieces, no more than about five minutes each, and they'll all be taken from the company's standard repertoire, which means you'll already be familiar with them since, of course, you'll have spent the whole of your first year learning them!"

My mind quickly ran over what we'd learnt, trying to decide what I'd most like to do. Not that I had any choice, but just last term we'd learnt the Dance of the Little Swans from *Swan Lake*. I wouldn't mind being a Little Swan!

Mr Leonardo read out from his list. Three of the boys were to do the Trepak from Nutcracker. Four of the girls – Mei, Caitlyn, Roz and Chloe – were to do the Dance of the Little Swans. (I swallowed. I might have known Ms Hickman wouldn't let me be a Little Swan! She probably still had it in for me. Everyone said she bore grudges.)

Mr Leonardo went on through the list. I waited eagerly for my name. Alex and Oliver – Tiffany, Finn – Amber, Giorgio… what about me? What was I supposed to be dancing?

"Finally," said Mr Leonardo, "Maddy and Nico –"

My heart thumped. At last!

"I know you haven't yet actually learnt any of the dances from *Fiesta* but as you're both quick studies we thought it might be fun if you did the Fandango. It's only very short and it would be something a bit different. What do you think? Are you up to it?"

I nodded so hard I thought my head would go flying off! Nico turned and gave me a huge grin.

"*Your* sort of thing." Tiffany mouthed the words at me across the studio. She probably thought she was getting back at me for what I'd said about her and Dad's bendy ballet. As if I'd been having a go at her! I'd only been telling it like it was. She's a really strong dancer but cold and glittering, like a splinter of ice. I like to think I have a bit more warmth than *that*. She was right, though, when she said that *Fiesta* was my kind of thing. It is exactly my kind of thing! Very fast and furious and exciting. And *passionate*. It's what I love about Spanish dancing: it is never just about technique. It is full of real emotion.

I felt my face break into a big happy beam. *This*, I thought, *was going to be a really good term!*

Chapter Two

There are some people who think that being ballet students we don't have to suffer normal school-type lessons such as maths and geography. They have this cosy picture of us dressed in our tights and leotards doing nothing but dance, dance, dance all day long. I wish! Not that I actually mind doing ordinary lessons. I really enjoy art and English. It's true I don't much care for maths, but that's probably only because I'm not very good at it. I would willingly not ever have to solve an equation again for the rest of my life! But we have to do what Dad calls "the academic stuff" to make sure we're properly rounded human beings. At least, that's what they tell us.

"There is absolutely no call," as Mrs Sinclair once bitingly informed us after we'd pulled faces at the prospect of a double period of maths, "no call whatsoever for a dancer to be ignorant."

She would say that, of course; she is Head of Academic Studies. What she didn't say, but what we all know, is that we need to be properly educated in case we don't make it as dancers and have to go out and find regular jobs like other people. It's what we all secretly dread. Caitlyn says it's one of her worst nightmares. "I'd just die!" Like Nico she had to fight really hard to get to ballet school. Not because she has a dad that disapproved but because her mum is a single parent and couldn't afford lessons.

I can understand why she worries, though in her case I honestly don't think there's any need. Mum, who is just about the most critical person I know, says that Caitlyn is a natural born dancer and that she has that elusive thing, star quality. I just don't think she quite realises it! Even after all this time she sometimes doubts her own abilities. She's not being mock modest, she genuinely *is* modest. Just as I'm not being boastful when I say that I'm actually well aware of my abilities. I know that I have a solid technique, a sense of the dramatic, and excellent *ballon* (meaning that I can jump very high and land very lightly). It's important, Mum always says, to know where your strengths lie. Those are my strengths! But of course you have to be aware of your weaknesses, as well, if only so that you can keep working on them. I, for instance, have had to accept that my line is not as pure as Caitlyn's and that I still have problems with *adage*. Gentle floating is not for me! I am far more of an *allegro* person. Quick footwork, fast turns. That's what I'm best at.

When it comes to ordinary lessons, English is what I'm best at. I have quite a vivid imagination, I really enjoy making up stories, but what I love most of all is being chosen to read aloud, like last term when we did *To Kill a Mockingbird* and I put on an American accent and everybody said it sounded just like the real thing. Even

Ms Turnbull, our English teacher, congratulated me. She said, "Well, done, Maddy! Very authentic." I can do French and German, as well. And, of course, Spanish! I love trying out different accents.

On our second day back we had English immediately following morning class. We always do an hour of class first thing, then academic studies for the rest of the morning. Dancing all afternoon! I was quite excited when Ms Turnbull told us that because of the company bringing *Romeo and Juliet* back into the repertoire, we were going to be reading the play that term. I knew the ballet almost from first step to last. I must have seen it at least five or six times on DVD, with wonderful dancers such as Margot Fonteyn and Alessandra Ferri in the role of Juliet – a part I would give anything to dance – but I had never actually seen the play.

"We won't be reading all of it," said Ms Turnbull. "Just the key scenes that tell the story, to prepare you for the ballet. I think, however, that we should start with the Prologue, as that sets the whole thing up. And as there are, of course, far more men's parts than women's, I think we'll give that to one of the girls."

She paused, her eyes roving round the class.

I sat forward, eagerly. *Me, me,* I thought. *Choose me!* I knew I sounded like I was back in Infants. It was all I could do not to wave my hand in the air! But I'd already glanced through the Prologue and I knew I could make sense of it. (Which of course you can't always in Shakespeare. Not without a struggle.)

"Let's have… Roz! You read it for us."

I sank back, disappointed. Roz is my friend but it has to be said she is absolutely useless when it comes to reading aloud. Especially Shakespeare. She turned and cast me this piteous look. She knows how passionate I am about anything to do with words. Plays, books, poetry. I do so hate it when they get all mashed and mangled! Still, the Prologue looked quite easy. Surely not even Roz could mess it up?

But she could! I listened in agony as she stumbled her way through.

"Two households, both alike in dignity,

In fair Venora –"

Verona, Verona! Had she never heard of Verona?

Roz stumbled on, obviously not understanding half of what she was saying.

"…from forth the fatal lions –"

I ground my teeth. Gently Ms Turnbull said, "I think, Roz, you'll find it's *loins*."

"Oh. Yes." Roz pulled a face. "Loins. *From forth the fatal loins of these two foes…*"

We finally managed to stagger as far as one of the scenes we knew so well from the ballet: a room in the Capulets' house, with Juliet's nurse, her mother (Lady Capulet) and Juliet herself. It's where Lady Capulet breaks the news to Juliet that she is to marry Paris – even though, of course, she's in love with Romeo. I sat up straight again, willing Ms Turnbull to notice me.

She did! But oh, guess what? She didn't want me to read Juliet, she wanted me to read the Nurse. Silly old fat Nurse! A role always taken by dancers who are nearing retirement. My only consolation was that Caitlyn was Juliet and she didn't actually have much to do in the scene. It was mainly me as the Nurse and Tiffany as Lady Capulet. Tiffany, to be fair, is quite a good reader. And the Nurse, as I quickly discovered, has a simply enormous long speech. (Thirty-three lines! I counted them.) Afterwards Caitlyn said that that was obviously why Ms Turnbull had chosen me to read the part.

"Nobody else could have done it!"

My cheeks went a bit sizzly at that. I hardly ever blush but even I can feel embarrassed on occasion. I muttered that I was sure Tiffany could have done it, which caused Amber to cry that Tiffany was absolutely brilliant! Which in turn obviously embarrassed Tiffany, cos instead of preening, as she normally would, she quickly said, "I'm nowhere near as good as Maddy. The way you got through that speech was amazing."

It is not like Tiffany to be so generous, especially

towards me. She finds it difficult, what with me having a mum and dad who both used to be members of the company, not to mention a brother who is one of their leading dancers. But then, when I think about it, I am perhaps not always very generous towards her. We simply don't get on! Still, if a person is good at something you can't not say so; that would be very small-minded. I'd found it really rewarding, doing a scene together. Not having to grit my teeth every few seconds or listen to Shakespeare's words being messed up. (Venora! I ask you.) It didn't alter the fact that what I still wanted more than anything was for Ms Turnbull to choose me as Juliet. We didn't have English again until later in the week. I reckoned that the next big scene we came to would be the balcony scene, where Romeo sneaks into the Capulets' orchard and sees Juliet appear on her balcony.

What light through yonder window breaks?
It is the east and Juliet is the sun.

I knew the words so well, even if I'd never seen the

play. I think they are probably words that most people know. Juliet's, too:

O Romeo, Romeo! Wherefore art thou Romeo?

I did so long to do the balcony scene! As soon as I arrived home I rushed upstairs to my bedroom to start practising it. I needed to be word perfect and to know the meaning of every line.

"So where are you off to in such a hurry?" demanded Mum.

"Got homework," I said.

"Oh?" Mum sounded agreeably surprised. I am not, as a rule, so eager! "Sean's going to be here in a minute. He's coming to have a word with Dad about the new ballet. I'm only telling you," said Mum, "because last time you complained about being kept in the dark and not having a chance to say hallo. But if you're going to be busy with homework—"

"No, no," I said. "I want to see him!"

I'm always happy to see Sean. I don't count school, where we practically have to behave like strangers. I do like to be able to talk to him sometimes, though usually when he calls round he claims he's in a mad rush and doesn't have a moment to spare. You have to catch him at just the right time and practically beg for an appointment. In spite of that, we do actually get on really well. Caitlyn, with her mad hero worship, used to be horrified at all the bad mouth she says I give him. But it's no more than he gives me! It's our idea of fun. He might be an important person in the company, but he's far from being grand. He is really quite easy-going, so long as you don't try interfering in his life like I did last term when he and Danny temporarily split up and everyone warned me not to get involved, only I did anyway, cos that's the sort of person I am, rushing in where (Dad says) angels fear to tread. Sean got quite mad at me, just like Jen had told me he would. It was worth it in the end, though, when he and Danny got back together. Sean even apologised for chewing me out.

I leaned over the banisters and called down to Mum. "Let me know before he goes!"

"Yes, all right," said Mum. "Just get on with your homework! I'm glad to know you're being so conscientious for once."

It's easy to be conscientious when you care deeply about something. I don't honestly care very much at all about maths or geography, which was our official homework for that evening. Usually I just do enough to scrape by. But I suddenly cared so much about being picked to read Juliet that it almost hurt. I wouldn't be able to bear it if Ms Turnbull chose one of the others and they messed it up!

I turned to the balcony scene and settled down on my bed to read it. Some of Romeo's speeches were rather long, so I mostly skipped through those and concentrated on Juliet. I did hope, if I got chosen – fingers crossed! – I really did hope that whoever was picked as Romeo would be able to make proper sense of all his words. Maybe it helped that I'd seen the ballet so many times. I not only knew the story and all the characters but even when I came across words I'd never met before I was mostly able to work out what Shakespeare was saying.

I became so engrossed that I almost forgot I was in my bedroom, sitting cross-legged on the bed. I really felt that I was Juliet, standing on my balcony in the moonlight, exchanging forbidden words with my beloved Romeo.

Oh, Romeo, Romeo, wherefore art thou Romeo?

I actually jumped when I heard someone tapping at my bedroom door. For a moment I thought that Nurse had arrived and that I'd been caught out! And then a voice said, "Mads? OK if I come in?"

The door opened a crack and Sean's head appeared. "Mum said you wanted to see me?"

"Oh. Yes!" I sat up straight against my pillows.

"So." Sean closed the door. "What can I do for you?"

I was about to admit that all I'd wanted was the chance to say hallo, but then I thought that maybe, if he was in a good mood and not in his usual rush…

"Well? Speak!"

"I don't suppose you could spare a few minutes?" I said. "Or are you in a hurry?"

"Not specially. Why?"

"D'you think you could read a bit of Shakespeare with me?"

He sighed. "If I must."

I said, "*Please?*"

"All right, all right! Anything to oblige. What are we reading?"

"*Romeo and Juliet*. The balcony scene."

"Oh." He sat down next to me on the bed. "Slurpy lurv!"

"It's not!" I was indignant. "It's beautiful!"

"You think?"

I flapped at him with my Penguin *Shakespeare*. "You know your trouble?" I said. "You are just *so* unromantic."

"Yup! That's me."

"*Romeo and Juliet* is one of the world's greatest love stories."

"Yeah, yeah!"

"I don't know how Danny puts up with you. If I were him I'd—"

"Well, you're not, so just get on with it. *Romeo, Romeo—*"

"But you've got a great long speech before Juliet comes in."

"*Soft what light through yonder window breaks it is the east and Juliet is the sun blah blah blah...*do you really expect me to wade through all that?"

"Maybe just the last few lines?"

"Let's skip straight to Juliet. Go on! Off you go."

"*Ay, me?*"

"No! Her first actual speech... *there.*"

He jabbed a finger on to the page. I immediately sprang up and made like I was standing on my balcony, staring out into the orchard.

"*O Romeo, Romeo! Wherefore art thou Romeo? Deny thy father and—*"

"Hang about, hang about!" Sean held up a hand.

"Gotta stop you right there. What exactly do you think she's saying?"

"Well…" I *knew* what she was saying. It was obvious! "Romeo, Romeo, where are you?"

"*Wrong.* What she's saying is, why oh why do you have to be called Romeo? If only he were called something else… in other words, if only he weren't a Montagu. Anything but a Montagu!"

He could obviously see the disbelief on my face.

"Look, there's a family feud, yes?" I nodded. "She's a Capulet: they're never going to let her marry a Montagu. So it's not Romeo, Romeo, wherefore *art* thou, Romeo, it's Romeo, Romeo, wherefore art thou *Romeo?*"

I was still doubtful. "Are you sure that's what it means?"

"I know that's what it means."

"How?" I said. "How do you know?"

"I know many things," said Sean, smugly.

"So… you're saying that *wherefore* means *why?*"

 37 ☆

"Back in Shakespeare's time," said Sean.

I found myself torn between relief that at least he had told me so that I wouldn't make an idiot of myself if I was chosen to read Juliet, and a feeling of annoyance that Sean, who didn't even like the play, obviously understood it better than I did.

"If you want to know the truth," he said, "the last time the company did the ballet was when I'd just started at the school and we all had to read the play and every single one of us got it wrong. Including me. That make you feel better?"

I nodded, gratefully. "What I don't understand," I said, "is why you don't dance Romeo?"

"I will, I will! Probably next season."

"It would make Caitlyn ever so happy. It really upsets her when Mercutio gets killed."

"That's one of my favourite bits!"

Cheekily I said, "Yes, I saw you staggering about, hamming it up." I stumbled off across the bedroom floor, writhing and choking and clutching at myself in agony.

"Honestly, the nerve of it," said Sean. "It asks me to give up my valuable time reading through some piece of romantic rubbish—"

"*That's* why you don't dance Romeo," I said. "You're obviously terrified of showing emotion!"

"Button it," said Sean. "Any more smart mouth and I'll leave you to get on with it by yourself. Start again, and try to make better sense of it this time."

My hard work paid off! Two days later, when we had English again, Ms Turnbull chose me to read Juliet. By then I knew the scene so well I could have done it without the book. Oliver, who was reading Romeo, stumbled a bit but I pretended to myself that that was because he was hiding in the Capulets' orchard, where he was in danger of being discovered at any moment. Maybe even by the vengeful Tybalt.

Afterwards Ms Turnbull thanked me for reading so well. She said I'd really brought Juliet to life.

"And congratulations for getting the first line right...

Romeo, Romeo, wherefore art thou Romeo? It's the first time I've ever known anyone do so!" And then, since everybody was looking puzzled: "It doesn't mean what you probably all think it means. Tell them, Maddy! What is Juliet saying?"

"She's saying, *why oh why do you have to be called Romeo?*"

I managed to do it without blushing. It might have been Sean who'd set me right, but I thought I should be allowed to take *some* credit. I had, after all, put in a lot of effort, reading the scene over and over and over again, which I didn't think anyone else had. I just wished there was someone I could tell about it. Mum, Dad, Sean... *Hey, guess what? Ms Turnbull thanked me for reading so well. She said I really brought Juliet to life!*

They would all be polite about it – well, Mum and Dad would be. Sean would probably claim it was all thanks to him. But none of them would truly be able to understand how important it was. How much it meant to me! I could only hug it to myself and bask in a warm glow of satisfaction.

Chapter Three

Almost before we knew it, Outreach Day was upon us. I couldn't believe how quickly the weeks had passed! They seemed to have whizzed by. Nico and I had been rehearsing every possible moment that we could, either with Mr Leonardo or by ourselves. We were both determined to live up to our reputation of being quick studies, plus we really did want to demonstrate how exciting ballet could be. I kept thinking of Chloe's friend Dominic who had complained that it was "all pink and pretty". Nobody, but nobody, could say that about our Fandango! I was so glad, now, that that was what Mr Leonardo had picked me for, rather than a Little Swan. The Little Swans were cute, all dancing together on pointe, with linked arms, their heads bobbing up and down, but I could see that maybe, for the boys, it wouldn't be macho enough. Not if they were into football, which most boys seem to be.

We all assembled in Studio One: sixteen of us dancers and twenty Year Eight pupils from the local school, mostly girls, though at a quick glance I counted seven boys among them. It was a comfort to know that they'd all volunteered and hadn't been forced into coming, so hopefully that meant they would be enthusiastic.

First off we did half an hour of class, as planned. Mr Leonardo, who was the teacher taking us, asked if any of our visitors felt like having a turn at the barre. Two of the girls volunteered. One of them had obviously had a few ballet lessons and was anxious to show what she could do. The other one overbalanced attempting a plié and collapsed into embarrassed giggles. I thought it was quite brave of her to have tried. Pliés may look simple but they're a bit more than an ordinary knees-bend. As she had discovered!

When we'd demonstrated what we did in class – *every single day of our working lives*, as Mr Leonardo impressed upon everyone – we prepared for our individual pieces. The Little Swans, the Trepak, the Czardas from *Coppelia*, and last of all Nico and me doing our Fandango. The visitors sat at one side of the studio, giving us plenty of room in the centre. At the end of every piece there was loud applause. At the end of the Trepak two of the boys actually started drumming on the floor with their feet, which brought an angry "Sh!" from their teacher, though I'm sure they were only doing it to show their appreciation.

When we'd all finished Mr Leonardo said he hoped everyone had enjoyed themselves and might feel inspired to go and see an actual performance some time in the future.

"And now, to thank you for being such a generous audience, may we offer you all some refreshments? Maddy, lead the way! Show our guests into the Green Room."

Next door, in the Green Room, there were glasses of fruit juice and plates of cookies all ready and waiting. I thought we were probably supposed to mingle and chat, but for the first few minutes we all tended to gather in separate corners. After a bit I couldn't help noticing that one of the boys kept sending glances towards me, or maybe towards Caitlyn, as we were standing together. I was just thinking that I should probably go and say something to him when he broke away from the others and actually came over to us.

Wanting to be friendly I said, "So what did you think? Did you enjoy it?"

"I loved the little baby swans," he said. "I thought that was really sweet! And the Russian stuff, that was pretty cool. I wasn't so keen on the other thing. I don't know how to pronounce it. That Kzardas thing."

"Chardash," said Caitlyn. "It's pronounced Chardash."

"Yeah! That one. I didn't care for that so much."

I could see Caitlyn opening her mouth to ask him why, but I jumped in ahead of her.

"What about the Fandango?" I said.

"Ah, yes! The Fandango…"

The way he said it, *fan-dan-go*, with a slight foreign lilt, made me wonder if perhaps he might speak Spanish. Even *be* Spanish. Eagerly I said, "What did you think of it?"

"Maddy's brilliant at anything Spanish," said Caitlyn.

I knew she was only trying to be supportive but I didn't want him saying nice things just because he felt he had to. Not that I could seriously believe he wouldn't have liked it. Everybody liked our Fandango! Mr Leonardo had said it was one of the best things me and Nico had ever done.

"The Czardas is a bit formal," I said. "Spanish is more expressive."

He nodded earnestly. "Yes!" he said. "That's what I thought."

I frowned. He was making it sound like he'd been disappointed. That it hadn't been as expressive as he thought it should have.

"Didn't you enjoy it?" said Caitlyn.

Very seriously he said, "That's what I wanted to talk to you about."

There was a pause. Caitlyn and I stood waiting. I said, "So?"

He shuffled, uncomfortably.

"You might as well tell us," I said.

"OK." He swallowed. "To be honest it didn't really seem very Spanish."

What? I felt so shocked I couldn't immediately think of anything to say. *Not very Spanish?* What on earth was he talking about? I was just struck completely dumb. Of the two of us, Caitlyn was the first to recover her powers of speech.

"Have you ever actually seen any Spanish dancing?" she said.

"I've seen loads!" He didn't seem to be boasting; just anxious for us to know.

"So who have you seen?" demanded Caitlyn.

He said, "I don't remember their names or anything

but I spent the whole of last summer staying with my gran. She lives over there, and there was dancing going on all the time, in the clubs and the cafes, everywhere! It was just, like, amazing, you know? Like you said, really expressive. Really wild. Full of emotion, like –"

To our utter astonishment he suddenly threw up his arms and started stamping, and clicking his fingers. Heads turned to see what all the noise was about. Someone giggled. Me and Caitlyn just stared, coldly. I thought honestly, some people! It was almost unbelievable. Thinking he could teach *us* about Spanish dancing. What a show-off!

"See what I mean?" He snapped his fingers and stamped even louder. "That's what I thought it was going to be!"

I felt like saying, "What? An undisciplined mess?" I didn't, of course, because it would have been rude, and even though he'd been rude to us first he was still our guest. Still, he obviously felt our hostility. Not surprising! Waves of it were coming at him both from me and from Caitlyn.

"I'm sorry," he said. "I was just trying to explain."

"You obviously don't know very much about dancing," said Caitlyn.

He hung his head. "I don't really know anything."

Well, I thought, that was plain to see.

"What I *think* you were trying to show us," said Caitlyn, "was Flamenco. What we do here is ballet."

"There does happen to be a difference," I said.

"Oh." He was looking a bit ashamed, now, and so he ought. The nerve of it! Teaching *us*. "I'm so stupid, I shouldn't have said anything. I hadn't realised. When it said *Fandango* I thought it meant like I saw in Spain. I guess ballet's more sort of…"

He hesitated. Dangerously, Caitlyn said, "More sort of what?"

"Well! Sort of… softer?"

Caitlyn said, "*Softer?*"

"Prettier!"

"Prettier," said Caitlyn.

Growing desperate he said, "Flamenco's a bit more

like tap dancing, maybe?" He looked at us, hopefully. "My sister does tap dancing."

"I do the splits," I said.

It was one of those smart remarks that don't actually mean anything. It sounded good, though! And it totally confused this idiotic boy. *Daring* to stand up in a room full of ballet students and do his pathetic clumsy stamping!

"I do think it's extraordinary," he mumbled, "all those exercises you have to do."

I thought *Yes, just to be pretty!*

"It must make you really fit."

He was trying so hard it was embarrassing. I think it came as a relief to all of us when his teacher finally called out that it was time to go. We parted company as politely as could be. *Thank you for inviting us* and *thank you for coming* and *I did enjoy it, honestly!* Caitlyn said after they'd left that she'd almost started to feel sorry for him. She can never stay cross with anyone for long.

"I'm sure he didn't really mean to be rude."

"Just didn't know what he was talking about," I said.

"At least he was trying to show an interest. And he did like the little baby swans!"

Crushingly I said, "Everybody likes the little baby swans."

You couldn't go wrong, being a baby swan.

"I do think he meant well, though," said Caitlyn. He just didn't realise that when you get Spanish dancing in a ballet it's not as –"

She waved a hand, searching for the right word. I looked at her, rather hard. Don't say *she* was going to upset me?

"Not as *raw* as Flamenco." She brought it out triumphantly.

"Just pretty," I said.

"Not pretty! More... balletic."

"You mean all pink and pretty."

Caitlyn looked at me reproachfully. "Now you're just being silly."

Maybe I was but his words still rankled. *Not very*

Spanish. Too soft. Too pretty. Nico and I had been so proud of our Fandango!

Nico, all unaware, grinned and said, "Looks like you've got an admirer! That guy that was talking to you? You obviously made an impression!"

I wished I could have told him that *we* had made an impression. As it was, I couldn't even bring myself to say that it was Caitlyn and the Little Swans that had so impressed him. I certainly wasn't going to tell him that my so-called admirer didn't think our Fandango was very Spanish. Not after we had put so much into it!

I brooded for the rest of the day. I was still brooding even as we made our way home that afternoon. A bunch of us always walked up to Waterloo together. As a rule I was one of the most talkative – mouth on a stick is what Sean calls me – but for once I couldn't rouse myself to join in. The words kept racing round my head: *not very Spanish.*

Caitlyn obviously guessed that it was preying on my

mind. I'd only been home about ten minutes when she rang me, all bright and bouncy and determined to cheer me up.

"Guess what I'm doing?" she said.

Grudgingly I said, "What?"

"I'm watching *Romeo and Juliet* on YouTube!"

I said, "So?"

"I'm watching the fight scene."

"With who?"

"No one! It's just m— oh!" She giggled. "Sorry! It's Fonteyn and Nureyev."

I said, "OK." It was a classic performance, but why was she ringing to tell *me*?

"I just wanted to let you know," said Caitlyn, "that that silly boy is utterly and totally *wrong*."

She said she couldn't imagine anything less soft or less pretty than Tybalt and Mercutio slashing at each other with swords and Mercutio getting run through. She said, "I think *you* ought to watch it."

"I've watched it about a thousand times," I said.

"So go and watch it again! Honestly, it'll stop you dwelling."

I said, "I'm not dwelling."

"You so are!" said Caitlyn. "You've been dwelling all day. Go and look it up on YouTube."

"Got it on a DVD," I said.

"Well, watch the DVD, then!"

In the end I did what she said. I brought my laptop downstairs and curled up on the sofa and started binge-watching on YouTube, one performance after another, desperately trying to see them through the eyes of all those people who thought ballet was too soft. Too pink and pretty. Mostly, much to my relief, I found myself agreeing with Caitlyn. Who could possibly think there was anything pink and pretty about two men fighting each other? Not to mention one of them actually dying. But then, just every now and again, I would have a little twinge of doubt and wonder if maybe it was all a bit too… well, balletic! They might be fighting but they were still dancing. They were still part of a ballet.

Maybe, I thought, *I should try watching the same scene from the play and see if there was any difference?*

Dad came in as I was about to start on version number three: the Royal Shakespeare company.

"What are you goggling at?" he said. He peered over my shoulder. "Oh! Pinky and Perky."

I said, "*Da-a-a-d!*"

"Sorry, sorry!" He flung up his hands as a sign of surrender. "*The Greatest Lurv Story Ever Told!*"

"Well, it is," I said. And why speak in that stupid mock-American accent? What was *wrong* with the men in my family? First Sean, now Dad! Had they no romance?

Dad was peering again, over my shoulder. "Why are you watching the play, by the way, rather than the ballet?"

"I'm making comparisons," I said.

"Oh, the ballet wins hands down," said Dad. "It's the ballet every time."

It was only what I would expect Dad to say. Or Mum. Or Sean.

"You don't think, sometimes," I said, "that ballet is a bit too… soft?"

Dad said, "*Soft?*"

"Well! Sort of pink and… pretty."

"I'll give you pink and pretty!" said Dad. He leaned forward and typed something into YouTube. "How about that?"

"Oh!" I said. "It's your bendy ballet."

I watched as a series of sinewy figures twisted and writhed across the screen.

"You think that's pink and pretty?" said Dad.

I thought, to be honest, that it was a bit weird. Clever, but weird.

"I was thinking more of traditional stuff like… *Sylphides?*"

"I'd call that beautiful rather than pretty," said Dad. "Don't confuse the one with the other."

"OK! What about peasant dances?"

"Mm… I guess some could be described as pretty. But always remember," said Dad, "even prettiness is the product of constant slog, not to mention blood, sweat and tears. As you very well know!"

I did very well know. Only the other day I'd taken my pointe shoes off at the end of class to find two of my toes rubbed almost raw where blisters had burst. Dancers' feet are not a pretty sight! And at some stage or another we all suffer from aches and pains. It's an inescapable part of being a dancer. We're used to it and we don't complain. It is just rather discouraging when we go through so much only to be told that the end result is nothing more than pink and pretty!

"Cheer up," said Dad. He patted my shoulder. "I'll make a ballet for you one day... and I promise it won't be either pink or pretty!"

"But it will have a story, won't it?" I pleaded.

"You want a story?" said Dad.

He was teasing me; like wanting a story was childish. What was wrong with dancing simply for the sake of dancing? In some of Dad's ballets you do just that. Abstract ballets, he calls them. But what I wanted was a ballet where I could act, as well as dance. Ballets like *Romeo and Juliet*. That was my sort of ballet! I had always loved acting, ever since I could remember. I never had the chance when I was at school – ordinary school, I mean. It was so frustrating! I used to plead with Miss Lucas every term to let me have a speaking part, but it was always "Oh, no, Maddy! You're our little dancer."

"Don't worry," said Dad. "You want a story, I'll give you a story!"

"Something dramatic," I said. I already had visions of headlines in the dance magazines: RISING ACTRESS IN THE BALLET WORLD! BALLET STAR POACHED BY NATIONAL THEATRE!

"You'll get what you're given," said Dad.

"So long as it's something I can get my teeth into!"

Dad just shook his head and laughed. That's the trouble with my family: they don't always take me seriously.

Chapter Four

Romeo was back in the company's repertoire. It had had its premiere and all the critics had been loud in their praise. One, in a ballet magazine, had even singled out the fight scene between Tybalt and Mercutio for special mention.

"*High drama.*" Caitlyn pointed triumphantly at the review. "*Keeps you on the edge of your seat no matter how many times you may have seen it before or how well you know the outcome. See?* I told you so!"

"We can judge for ourselves on Wednesday," I said.

All of us first and second year students had been invited to a mid-week matinee. It was part of the Outreach programme, with special concessions for local schools. Someone said that *Romeo and Juliet* was on the syllabus and that most schools were doing it for GCSE.

"I hope that stupid boy's not going to be there," I said. "Cos if he is, and if he makes any more of his idiotic remarks, I shall say something."

"He couldn't possibly make idiotic remarks about *Romeo and Juliet*," said Caitlyn. "Certainly not the fight scene!" She pointed again at the review. "*Keeps you on the edge of your seat. I'm really excited! Aren't you?*"

I was looking forward to it but I wouldn't have said that I was excited, exactly. I don't think any of us would have said we were excited. Only Caitlyn! She is always totally open about her emotions. It doesn't seem to occur to her that other people – people like Tiffany, for example – might not find it cool. Sometimes I think she's a bit naive; other times I can't help but admire her honesty.

"I just hope," I said, "that you'll manage to keep your eyes open."

She looked at me, puzzled. "Why wouldn't I?"

I said, "Well, you were the one that told us you couldn't bear to watch! When Mercutio got killed? You said you couldn't bear it!"

"Oh, that was just me being silly," said Caitlyn. "I didn't really mean it. Of course I'm going to watch! I watched the other day, didn't I, on YouTube?"

"Yes, but that was no one," I said.

She giggled. "Only one of the stars of the Bolshoi Ballet!"

"And who is he compared with the Beloved?" I clasped my hands to my chest. "Sean, Sean, wherefore art thou Sean?"

"Maddee!" She pushed at me. "I'm over all that."

"Oh, you are such a liar!" I jeered.

I don't mean to be cruel but she is just so easy to tease. Plus I believe that secretly she enjoys it. I think if I had a crush on someone I would probably bask in the very mention of his name, though as I have never had more than the tiniest little twinge it's difficult to be certain. The closest I ever came was when I was eleven and Jen took me to see a Spanish dance company and I fell a little bit in love with the lead dancer and hugely in love with everything Spanish. Which was why that stupid boy and his ignorant remarks had upset me so much!

Fortunately, on Wednesday, he wasn't there, or if he was he kept well away. Caitlyn said it would be a pity if he hadn't come because it would have proved to him how tense and dramatic ballet could be.

"I wish we could see the play some time," I said. "You know, just to compare?"

"I don't think I could love it as much as I love the ballet," said Caitlyn.

"I don't know," I said. "It would be interesting."

"I suppose."

"You have to have an open mind," I said. "There's other ways of telling stories besides dancing."

"It's not just the dancing," said Caitlyn. "I'd miss the music and the scenery and the costumes."

"You'd still get scenery and costumes," I said. "Plus you'd get Shakespeare's words! Juliet is a part I would so love to do."

"You mean, to dance?" said Caitlyn.

I thought about it.

"Both," I said. I had been dancing so long I couldn't really imagine any other sort of life; but I did know that acting had to be a part of it as well. "I'm going to do both!" I said.

As we were standing on the platform at Waterloo later on, waiting for the Tube, I noticed a girl looking at us. She seemed to be trying to make up her mind whether she knew us or not. She was with a group of other kids, boys and girls, all wearing the same uniform: red tracksuits with a little logo that I couldn't quite make out. I didn't recognise the school it belonged to but it wasn't the one that had visited us on Outreach day. So why was she studying us so intently? Did she think she knew me? I certainly didn't know her! I'd never seen her in my life before. I'd have remembered if I had cos she was actually quite striking. She had very long, very thick blonde hair. Dead straight, like it had been ironed. I caught her eye and tilted my head, like, *Do we know each other?* It was all the invitation she needed. She immediately detached herself from the group and came over.

"Excuse me for asking," she said, "but you're Sean O'Brien's sister, aren't you?"

I felt Caitlyn quiver beside me. Mention of the Beloved!

Guardedly I said, "Yes?"

Almost always when people ask me if I'm Sean's sister it's because they want me to get his autograph for them. It can be quite tiresome, which is why I probably didn't sound very inviting. Not that it seemed to bother her. She just gave me this big grin and said, "I knew you had to be! *They* –" she nodded in the direction of her friends – "said I was imagining it, but I knew I was right! We've just been to see *Romeo and Juliet* and I noticed you sitting there, right in front of us. I knew he had a sister who was at ballet school. I once saw a photo of you in a magazine. You and your mum and dad and your brother. I recognised you at once! There is a sort of resemblance."

"You mean she looks like her photo?" said Caitlyn.

"No!" The girl gave a happy peal of laughter. "Like her brother! You can tell they're related. I hope you didn't mind me asking?" she added, anxiously. "It's just they all think I'm mad."

"That's OK," I said.

At least she hadn't begged for an autograph. *Yet.* There was still time. But I was pleased she thought there was a resemblance between me and Sean. Jen has always said we're quite alike as people – well, perhaps *complained* would be a more accurate way of putting it. She says we're both madly overconfident and don't respond well to authority. It's true we aren't goody goodies! But I had never really thought we looked much like each other, considering Sean has dark hair while mine is a kind of reddish brown, not to mention the fact that my face is rather distressingly *round* – though maybe, with any luck, not quite as round as it used to be. Just the other day I'd looked in the mirror and thought *Yay! I'm getting cheekbones.*

This girl had cheekbones. She had good long legs, too.

"Are you a dancer?" I said.

She said, "No, I'm an actress. Well, training to be. We're doing scenes from *Romeo and Juliet* for our end-of-term assessment – the play, that is – so we thought it would be interesting to see what the ballet was like."

"Did you enjoy it?" I said.

"Loved it! All of it."

"So which do you prefer? The ballet or the play?"

"Mmm…" She thought about it. "I s'pose I'd have to go with the play, but that's cos I'm an actor. I like having lines! But you're a dancer so I expect you'd probably choose the ballet."

"Absolutely," said Caitlyn, suddenly coming to life.

The girl said, "Well, but it's only natural, isn't it? You

express yourself through dance, I express myself through words. It doesn't mean one's any better than the other. Just different."

The train came in and we all stepped on, in a bunch. I sat next to the actress girl, leaving Caitlyn to stand by herself. I knew it wasn't very loyal of me, her being my best friend and all. I should have stayed with her, but there were just so many things I wanted to know. So many questions I wanted to ask! I could still have gone on asking them even when we arrived at our stop. Reluctantly, I stood up.

"This is where we get off. I'm really glad I met you!"

"Me too," said the girl. "I'm Steph, by the way."

"I'm Maddy," I said, though she probably knew that. "We might bump into each other again, maybe?"

"I'd like that," said Steph. And then, as I was about to get off: "You're welcome to come and watch our Shakespeare scenes!"

"I'd love to," I said.

"Just check out the website, it's all there!"

I jumped off the train and hurried to catch up with Caitlyn. She was already halfway up the platform. She might have waited for me!

"That was so interesting," I said. "She was telling me how she goes to this drama school?"

"Yes, I got that," said Caitlyn. "They'd just been to the ballet and she recognised you. I heard all that."

"Yes, but she was telling me, the place she goes to... Rosemount Stage School? It's just one stop away! Right near us."

Caitlyn looked at me as if to say, *So what?*

"I never realised," I said. "I had no idea it was there!" When it comes to ballet schools I know practically every one in the whole of London. I know who teaches at them, I know people who have studied at them, I know what Mum thinks of them. I didn't know very much at all about stage schools.

"Did you see their little logo?" I said. "On their sweatshirts? The smiley face and the sad one? She told me they're the masks of tragedy and comedy!"

Caitlyn said, "Oh?" She sounded less than impressed. I'd obviously upset her.

"I didn't mean to ignore you," I said. "But they're doing *Romeo and Juliet*!"

"Scenes," said Caitlyn.

I said, "Yes, and guess what? She's doing the balcony scene!"

My scene.

"She said last year," I told Caitlyn, "she got a part in a pantomime. In *town*. The school arranges auditions for them. They act like they're an agent. They *encourage* them."

Caitlyn pulled a face. "Would you actually *want* to be in a pantomime?"

"Wouldn't mind," I said. "I'd like to be in *something*."

"So maybe we'll be used in *Nutcracker*. Surely you'd rather be in that than in –" she waved a hand – "*Babes in the Wood*?"

"Oh, well, yes, of course," I said. "But I don't see why we couldn't do both. Steph's only the same age as us and she's already been in loads of things! They start them off really young. Steph's even done commercials."

"What, like advertising babies' nappies?" said Caitlyn.

Oh, boy! She was *really* mad at me.

"Look, I'm sorry I didn't introduce you," I said. "I will next time."

"You're going to see her again?" said Caitlyn.

"I mean if we happen to bump into each other. She only lives a few stops away. She's really nice," I said. "You'd like her."

Caitlyn just grunted. I suppose maybe I'd have felt a bit excluded if she'd struck up a conversation with some strange girl and just ignored me. But then I wouldn't let myself be ignored! I'd make sure I joined in.

I arrived home to find Mum on her way out.

"Can't stop," she cried. "Got a four-thirty class. Get yourself something to eat, your dad should be home any minute. Oh, and Jen's here, by the way. She said she'd hang on because she knows you like to see Thomas."

I'd been feeling a bit guilty about Caitlyn, but I perked up when I heard that. I love seeing Thomas! Tiny little babies I am not so keen on as they always look rather breakable and don't really do very much. But now that Thomas was a toddler we got on just fine. We are great chums. He makes me laugh! I specially enjoy reading him stories and putting on all the different voices.

I found Jen downstairs in the basement — what we call "the den". Thomas was curled up beside her, sucking his thumb and looking angelic. I said, "Thomas! My man!" He immediately sprang into life, squealing "Gimme five!" and waving his hand. It kills me when he does that! It was Sean who taught him. I don't think he quite gets what it means, but he knows it amuses us.

"Ah, good," said Jen. "I was hoping you'd arrive. Now I can tell you my news!"

"What's that?" I said. Could she be planning a return to the company? Lots of dancers do pick up their careers again when they've had babies. Mum did, twice. She only stopped when I came along, but she always says it was about time: "You can't go on forever." But Jen was still young! She could have another ten years ahead of her.

Eagerly I bounced myself down on to the sofa, next to Thomas. "Are you going to make a comeback?"

"What? No!" She laughed. "I'm going to have another baby!"

I said, "Oh." And then, thinking that maybe you were meant to say something a bit more meaningful when your older sister tells you she's pregnant, I gave a high-pitched squeak and went, "*Oh!*"

"I just dropped by to tell Mum."

"What did she say?"

"She said, *Well, if you've got one I suppose you might just as well have two…* typical Mum!"

"You know she's crazy about Thomas," I said. How could anyone not be? He is such a happy little boy! Always smiling, always gurgling with laughter. "She's obviously forgiven you your sins!"

"You mean she's forgiven me for leaving the ballet?"

Jen pulled a face. "It is a sort of sin in this family, isn't it? How can I bear to exist as just a normal person?"

"Don't you ever miss it?" I said.

"I miss some of it... I miss the people. I miss the companionship. What I don't miss," said Jen, "is the daily grind."

"But doesn't life seem kind of... well! Empty?"

"How can it seem empty," said Jen, "when I have Thomas? He's the best thing that's ever happened to me!"

I couldn't help thinking how different we were. The best thing that could ever happen to me would be to dance the part of Juliet. Or, of course, to act it. One or the other!

Jen shook her head. "You don't get it, do you?"

I had to admit that I didn't. "See, I want to *do* things," I said.

She seemed amused. "You don't think that looking after a two-year-old is doing things?"

I crinkled my nose. I wasn't honestly sure that I did.

I mean, yes, it could be hard work – I supposed – but it wasn't like it was anything particularly special. After all, anyone could have a baby! I wanted to do something that was just *me*.

"Don't worry," said Jen. "You'll change!"

"Mum didn't," I said. "Even after she gave up dancing she still did things." The Yvette Anderson Academy of Dance is one of the most respected in the country.

"Mum is a very driven sort of person," said Jen. "We can't all be like that. I think I knew even while we were growing up that I was nowhere near as ambitious as Sean, for example."

"I'm ambitious," I said. "I'm not going to give up, ever!"

"Well, yes, that's what you say now. You'd be surprised how differently you can feel when you're a mum."

"Maybe I won't be a mum."

"Yes, and maybe you will, and then you'll understand what I'm talking about!"

I sighed. "It's all very unfair, isn't it? It's so much easier for men."

"You can say that again," agreed Jen. "If Sean ever became a dad he could just go right on dancing. It wouldn't interrupt his career for a second."

I giggled. "Just as well it's not likely to happen cos he'd make a really rotten job of it!"

"You think? He's brilliant with Thomas."

"That's cos he's only his uncle. It's easy, just being an uncle!"

"Still, it'd be a shame," said Jen. "Danny would make a really great dad."

"That's cos Danny's a very responsible sort of person."

"Sean could learn… and so could you!"

"Not me." I shook my head, vehemently. I felt very definite about it: I intended to *be* someone. Not famous, necessarily; but *someone*. Maddy O'Brien, dancer; Maddy O'Brien, actress. Not just Sean O'Brien's sister, but me, myself. *Me!*

Jen said, "Oh, you really are Mum's daughter, aren't you?"

Maybe, I thought, as a dancer I would always be Mum's daughter? Maybe if I stayed in ballet there could be no escaping it? Maybe there never had been any escaping it. Maybe my path had been mapped out from the very beginning. But paths had turnings! Sometimes you came to crossroads. Who knew what the future might hold?

"What are you thinking?" said Jen. "You have that look in your eye."

I said, "What look?"

"Like you're cooking something up!"

"Don't like cooking," I said. "When I'm Somebody I shall eat in restaurants every day of the week!"

"Well, that's a very worthy ambition, I'm sure." Jen pulled Thomas on to her lap and nuzzled him. "I think I'll just stick with my little guy here!"

Chapter Five

As soon as Jen left, I grabbed my laptop and put in *Rosemount Stage School*. I was curious to find out where it was, exactly. I clicked on *Contact* and the address came up: 44–46 Layton Road.

I knew Layton Road! A girl at my old school had lived there, at number 63. I'd once gone to a party she'd had, which meant I must have passed Rosemount without realising. I was suddenly filled with an urge to go and look at it. Just to see where it was that she went, this girl called Steph with the long blonde hair and striking looks. Even Caitlyn, mad at me though she was, could hardly deny Steph was beautiful.

According to the website the school ran two

programmes. One was for full-time students, one for part-time. I thought that Steph, from the way she'd been talking, must be full-time. Part-time students had classes on Friday evenings and all day Saturday. Singing, dancing, acting, musical theatre. Entry, it said, was by audition, even if you only wanted to go part-time. There was a little piece explaining that even though many of the students attending part-time were doing it for fun, rather than hoping to become professionals, they still had to prove "real and demonstrable talent".

The school, it went on, *will represent all students, be they full- or part-time, for the purposes of procuring professional engagements.*

In other words, pantomimes! Not to mention plays, and television, and Christmas shows. It must be so exciting, I thought, to be put up for a part in a show. It didn't happen at ballet school! Well, certainly not at ours. Ms Hickman would go stiff with outrage at the thought of one of her precious dancers being seen in anything as vulgar as a pantomime. Babette's Babes, who are pupils at a little local dance school, are forever kicking their legs about in *Mother Goose* or *Little Red Riding Hood*. Mum, of course, holds them in contempt. Mum is as bad as Ms Hickman. She is a total ballet snob. It's, like, *chorus work? Pah! Tap dancing? Pah!* Even modern dance is a little bit *pah!*

I looked again at the Rosemount website. Classes were held not only in acting but in musical theatre, tap, ballet, street and acrobatic. How Mum would curl her lip! She simply cannot see that there's more to life than perfect turn-out and the ability to do thirty-two *fouettés* without falling over. I loved the sound of acrobatic dancing! Street, too. I wondered if I could persuade Dad to do a street dance ballet. Mum would just groan and roll her eyes, but Dad's not as much of a snob as Mum is. He is at least willing to consider new ideas.

Dad came in as I was still poring over the website.

"What's that?" he said. "Anything interesting?"

"It's street dance," I said. I'd clicked on to the school's

picture gallery, showing photos of recent student productions.

"Mm." Dad leaned forward, studying the photo. "Looks like fun."

"You could do a street dance ballet," I said.

"Maybe I could. I'll bear it in mind."

This is what I mean about Dad: he is always open to new suggestions. I did wonder, though, if he would be quite so happy if I told him the sudden crazy idea that had just flashed across my brain: suppose I did an audition for Rosemount? Just an audition! I didn't actually want to go there. Well, obviously, I couldn't. Unless maybe part-time... but then we often had classes on a Saturday, so that wouldn't work. But I could still take the audition! It would at least tell me whether I was any good as an actress. That was all I wanted to know. Surely Dad would understand?

Dad might; maybe. Mum certainly wouldn't. She'd start on again like she had once before, about me not being committed enough. But I was committed! I just wanted to be able to act as well as dance. I'd once said this to Caitlyn, who'd pointed out that there wasn't anything to stop me doing both.

"Just think of all those big dramatic roles like Juliet, and Giselle, and that Spanish one you love... *El Amor Brujo!* Think of poor Giselle having her heart broken and going mad... tell me *that* doesn't need someone who can act!"

I knew she was right; but that was acting through dance. I wanted to know if I could act with words! Ms Turnbull had praised me for my reading of Juliet in class, but how would I measure up to people like Steph, who were as dedicated to drama as I was to ballet? Cos I *was* dedicated! It can't be wrong to experiment occasionally. *Expand your horizons.* That is what Dad's always saying: *Don't be afraid to try your hand at something new.* That was all I wanted to do! I didn't actually want to go to drama school. I mean, I obviously couldn't. Unless, perhaps...

"Dad?" I said. "You don't think—"

"Just a sec." Dad had put his glasses on and was studying the screen, intently. "That couple there —" he pointed — "have really got the hang of things! What is this? Some school or other?"

I said, "It's Rosemount Stage School."

"Oh, Rosemount! Yes, I know it. They've obviously got some talented kids. So what's your interest? You proposing to take up street dancing? That'd please your mother! Like you haven't already got enough on your plate. How are things, anyway? After that bit of trouble you had last term... everything OK?"

I said, "Yes, fine."

"Good! You had your mother really worried there for a while. I'll think about the street dance thing, by the way. I've logged it." He tapped his forehead. "It's all in there. I just need to wait for the right music to turn up... set things in motion."

I'd been on the point of asking Dad what he thought about me taking an audition — "Just to see if I could get in! I know I couldn't actually go there, unless maybe I could do it part-time. I could maybe do it part-time! Couldn't I, Dad? Couldn't I just do it part-time?" – but he'd disappeared before I could get the words out. It was probably just as well. Not even Dad was likely to approve of the idea. He might even mention it to Mum, and then I would be in deep trouble. *Again.* If I did decide to go ahead I would obviously have to do it in secret. Not tell a single solitary soul. Not even Caitlyn. It wouldn't be easy, but then things that are worth doing usually aren't, or so Mum is always telling me.

I thought as a first step I could at least go and look at the school. *That* wouldn't be easy, either. Layton Road might be only one stop away on the Tube, but when could I go without Caitlyn knowing? I couldn't do it in the morning, I wouldn't have time, and Caitlyn and I always travelled back together in the afternoon. She would wonder where I was off to, all by myself. I would have to think up some excuse, like… *You'd better go on without me, I've got an extra class?* That wouldn't work. Why would I be having an extra class? And if I said I was going to meet someone she'd want to know who, just like I'd want to know if it was the other way round. It is part of the problem when you are really close friends with someone: you both expect to share each other's secrets.

In the end I just suddenly came out with it as we were on the train, on our way home the next day.

"I'm going to stay on for another stop," I said. "I want to go and check out Steph's drama school. D'you feel like coming with me?"

"What, now?" said Caitlyn. She was already half out of her seat. "What d'you want to do that for?"

"Just curious," I said. "I want to see what it looks like."

The doors opened. Caitlyn hesitated.

I said, "You coming, or not?"

"Oh, all right." She sank back down. "If you're going, I suppose I might as well. But I still can't understand why you want to!"

"I told you," I said. "I'm curious."

 84 ☆

She shook her head, like, *I don't get it.*

"Do you actually know where it is?" she said, as we left the train at the next stop.

"Course I do! Layton Road. Just round the corner from the station. Girl at Coombe used to live there… Sophy Pringle? I went to one of her parties. I think she left just before you started."

We walked out on to the station forecourt and just for a moment my confidence deserted me. There seemed to be big wide roads going off in all directions! I'd only been there the once and then it was in a car. Things look different when you're on foot.

"So where do we go?" said Caitlyn.

I pointed. "That way! I think."

Caitlyn looked at me, doubtfully. "Are you sure?"

She really does make me very impatient at times. Growing a bit tetchy I said, "No, but if I'm wrong we can always ask. That's what tongues are for!"

I struck out, boldly, with Caitlyn dithering a few paces behind.

"You don't think we should just give up and go home?" she said.

I told her that she could if she wanted. *I* was going to find Layton Road.

I did, too! It was just where I'd remembered it, from all that time ago.

"And, look," I said, "there's the school!"

It was two old houses with a big board saying **"Rosemount Stage School, Principal: Mrs Arlene Ashworth**."

Caitlyn, rather sniffily, said, "It doesn't look like much."

"Nor does Mum's place," I said, "and that's one of the best ballet schools in the country. *And*," I reminded Caitlyn, "you once told me you used to go out of your way to walk past Mum's place just so you could look at it!"

"That's cos I was desperate to go there," said Caitlyn. "It was my big dream. You're not dreaming about going to that place! *Are* you? Maddy? You're not!"

I said, "Of course I'm not. Don't be silly! How could I?"

"Well, you couldn't," said Caitlyn.

"So there you are! I'm just interested. I told you!"

"Doesn't look like much to be interested in," said Caitlyn. "Looks a bit tatty to me."

"That's all you know," I told her. "Dad says they have some really talented kids and – oh! Look – there's Steph!"

She'd just appeared with a group of other girls and a couple of boys. I waved at her and she saw me and waved back. "Wait there, I'll come over!"

I felt Caitlyn plucking fretfully at my sleeve. "We really ought to be getting home."

I said, "Yes, all right, just give me a minute."

Steph had already detached herself from the group and was preparing to cross the road. It would be extremely rude to just walk away, and anyhow, why should I? Just cos Caitlyn had the hump!

"Hi, you two!" Steph arrived with a bound in front of us. "What are you doing here?"

"We just came to see an old school friend," I said.

"She used to live in this road, but we think perhaps she might have moved, don't we?" I turned to Caitlyn. "I remember, now, her mum and dad were talking about it."

"So why did we bother?" muttered Caitlyn.

"To *check*," I said.

Caitlyn said, "Oh. I see."

"It was ages ago," I explained to Steph. "I expect we should have rung first. See if she was still here." Brightly I added, "I didn't realise this was where your drama school was! I never noticed it before."

"It's been here for ages," said Steph. "Almost a quarter of a century. Mrs Ashworth started it when her daughter was five, and she must be at least thirty by now."

"CBS has been around since the 1950s," said Caitlyn.

"Oh, well, yes," said Steph. "That's one of the major schools. Rosemount's only tiny."

"But it's got some very talented pupils," I said. "According to my dad."

"Is that what he said?" Steph's face lit up. "I do think Mrs Ashworth's a really good teacher. Lots of her old pupils are in the biz. Some of them you've probably heard of. And her daughter's just got a part in a movie! Lines, and everything."

Caitlyn opened her mouth but I pushed at her, crossly. She gave me a reproachful stare.

"I was only going to *say*," she said, "that we should be getting home."

Reluctantly I said, "Yes, OK."

"Are you going to the Tube?" said Steph. "I'll come with you."

I knew Caitlyn wouldn't be pleased. She'd really taken against Steph, though I couldn't think why. She surely couldn't be jealous? I suddenly remembered that I hadn't done what I'd promised to do: I hadn't introduced her. Maybe that was why she was being so huffy.

"Steph, this is Caitlyn," I said. "We used to be at school together – I mean, ordinary school. Now we're in the same year at CBS."

Steph nodded. "I knew she had to be a dancer," she said. "You can always tell."

Well, I thought, *that* ought to please her. We set off, three abreast, for the station.

"How long have you been at Rosemount?" I said.

Steph said she'd started there when she was ten, just a couple of hours a week. "But I loved it so much my parents let me go full-time."

"Did you have to take an audition?" I said. "What did you do for it?"

"Sang a song—"

"Which one?"

"Something from *Polly*."

"Oh," I said, "I adore *Polly*! Which song was it?"

"'If I Had Three Wishes'."

"That's one of my favourites," I said.

"Mine, too!" Suddenly, without any warning, right there on the street, Steph opened her mouth and burst into song. She had quite a sweet voice, though nothing

★ 90 ☆

particularly special. *No better*, I thought, *than mine. I could sing something from* Polly!

"How about a speech? Did you have to do a speech?"

"Yup!" She nodded. "I did one I found in a book of audition pieces. Very dramatic! I had to break down and cry. Like this!"

Even as we watched, her mouth began to pucker, her lips quivered, and slowly the tears began to scrunch out of her eyes. I was impressed! How did she *do* that? Maybe it was some kind of technique that they taught you at drama school.

"That's amazing," I said.

She shrugged. "You do what you're best at. I'm best at being dramatic! How about you?"

"Oh, me, too," I said. "But if I was doing a speech I'd probably do Shakespeare."

"I might now," agreed Steph. "Now that we're putting on *Romeo and Juliet*. But I didn't really understand Shakespeare when I was only eleven. It's quite difficult."

"I love it!" I said. "I know you have to work at it but I do like to do things that are challenging."

We went on chatting as we stood on the platform waiting for our separate trains. Steph lived a few stops further up the line, in the opposite direction from me and Caitlyn, so I was hoping, as we said goodbye, that now she had me to herself again Caitlyn might cheer up a bit. Instead, almost accusingly, she said, "What were you talking about auditions for?"

"Just showing an interest," I said.

"You made it sound like you were thinking of taking one."

I crinkled my nose. Puzzled. "Why on earth would I want to do that? And anyway, how could I? And what would be the point?"

"Same as when you went ice skating?" said Caitlyn.

"Oh, that was just to prove I could do it."

She said, "Hm!" And then, "At least you don't need to prove you can act cos everyone knows that you can. Ms Turnbull said so."

I thought yes, but Miss Turnbull was only an English teacher. Not drama. I needed someone like Arlene Ashworth to tell me. *That* would be proof!

But that would mean taking an audition, and how could I? Without Mum or Dad or anyone knowing? Obviously I couldn't, so that was that. I would just have to put the idea out of my mind. I'd got into enough trouble last term! I couldn't afford to risk it again.

Chapter Six

I knew that I had to forget about it. Even just applying for an audition would be stupid, never mind actually going for one. If it ever got back to Mum or Ms Hickman I'd be in the deepest trouble. And how could I hope to do it without one or other of them finding out? I couldn't! So *just stop thinking about it. Right?*

Right.

All right, then! STOP.

Now.

I did my best. I really did! But still I couldn't quite bring myself to let go of the idea. I could feel all the time that it was lurking there, just waiting to spring out at me. Like at night I would wake up and find myself wondering what song I would sing, or what poem I would do. And then I would start singing songs in my head, or running through bits of poetry that I could remember from school. It was like it just jumped out at me without any warning. Even in the middle of class!

We had mime one afternoon with Mr McArthur. We always felt very privileged when Mr McArthur took us. He had been one of the company's leading dancers in Mum's time; he and Mum had even been partners for a while. Now he was a teacher at the school, though mostly he taught the senior pupils, taking them through the various corps roles in the company's repertoire. He was also regarded as an expert in mime, which I specially loved.

Some companies don't include mime in their ballets any more, which I think is a pity. I think it's amazing that you can use it to tell a story to audiences all over the world, knowing that everyone will understand it no matter what their native language is.

Mr McArthur was teaching us the mime from Act I

of *Swan Lake*, where Prince Siegfried meets Odette for the first time. I suppose, if it was printed out like a play script, it would look a bit odd:

Prince Siegfried to Odette: *You – fly away – no.*

In other words, as Mr McArthur explained (to those of us who mightn't know), "He's asking her, *please don't fly away*. OK? And then he says… *you – here – why*? And Odette says – all right, Maddy! You look as if you're bursting to tell us. What does Odette say?"

"She says, *I –*" I pointed to myself – "*am the Queen –*" miming a crown on top of my head – "*of all the Swans*," rippling my arms and taking special care to make them swan-like. When Mum was teaching me she was forever telling me to "Watch those arms!"

"Good," said Mr McArthur. "Thank you, Maddy. How about you, Nico? Care to tell us what Siegfried says?"

"*You –*" Nico pointed at me – "*are a queen, and I –*" pointing to himself – "*bow to you.*"

Slowly we worked our way through the complete

scene, showing how Odette tells Siegfried that "*over there is a lake of my mother's tears*", explaining to him how a wicked magician, von Rothbart, had turned her into a swan, but that "*if someone will marry me and promise to be true then I will be a swan no more.*"

Mr McArthur said, "Nice work, everybody! Maddy and Nico, that was excellent. Caitlyn, you have the most beautiful and expressive arms but remember! *I –*" he pointed a finger at himself – "*you –*" he flung out an arm – "*over there…* you're not telling the story to a little group of friends in your living room but to an audience of maybe a couple of thousand in a vast auditorium! So *be expansive*! The same with you, Mei. *Big gestures*. Tiffany, a little more feeling, if you please! We need the audience to do more than just understand what you're telling them, they have to be moved by the emotions that are behind the gestures. OK?"

Tiffany nodded and said, "Right," but I saw her pull a face as Mr McArthur turned away. She's not someone that likes to be criticised. I don't much like it, either, but I wouldn't pull a face. Even when Mum used to go on about my arms I never pulled faces. Just inwardly cringed!

Tiffany complained, afterwards, that mime belonged to the past and was a complete waste of time.

"I don't know why we bother with it any more... lots of companies don't. I mean, honestly... *you – here – why?* It's like talking to a six-year-old! It's just embarrassing. *And* it holds up the story!"

"Actually," said Roz, "it *tells* the story."

"Only if people can understand it, which most probably they can't."

"But it's easy," protested Caitlyn. "Even before I started taking lessons I could work out what most of it meant."

"Oh, genius," said Tiffany.

"No, but it's all logical! *I – you – swan – marry...* I love it!"

Rudely, Tiffany said, "You would! You love everything."

A hot tide of colour rose into Caitlyn's cheeks.

"The only reason you think it's a waste of time," I told Tiffany, "is because you're no good at it. You just don't have any feeling for it. It's like someone that's learnt French but can't speak it properly."

Tiffany gave me this look of intense dislike. She said, "You think you're so brilliant?"

"I think I'm better than you," I said. "At mime, that is."

"Yeah, you reckon you're this great actress. This great Shakespeare scholar, knows what it's all about." Tiffany clasped her hands to her bosom and put on a silly little girly voice: *"Romeo, Romeo, wherefore art thou Romeo?"*

It was my turn to go pink. With annoyance! Before I could say anything, my beloved Nico had spoken up for me. The boys usually stayed well clear of any spats between us girls, but Nico and I have this fierce loyalty to each other. It's what being partners is all about.

"Wanna make a bet?" he said. "*I bet* that in a few years' time Maddy's not only going to be one of the leading dancers in the company, she's going to be known as one of those dancers who can act as well as dance."

"And there aren't that many," said Chloe.

"Exactly." Nico nodded. "So! Just saying." He grinned at me as we made our way to Studio One for our next class.

"That told her!" he said.

"Did you –" I hesitated. "Did you really mean what you said? About me being able to act as well as I can dance?"

"Of course I did!" He looked at me in surprise. "You must know that you can."

That was when it sprang out at me again: if I could just go for an audition! Just an audition; that was all. Just to hear Arlene Ashworth confirm that Nico was right. It wasn't that I didn't trust him, but there was still this nagging doubt: how much did he actually know? He was a dancer. *I* was a dancer. Mrs Ashworth was the principal of a respected drama school. She was the expert!

On the train on the way home Caitlyn burbled excitedly

about the end-of-term recital that the second and third years traditionally gave. *Showtime!* For us second years it would be our very first public performance, so everyone was naturally starting to grow quite tense and anxious, wondering whether they would be entrusted with a solo or simply be part of an ensemble. We were all aware that a lot depended on what you were given to do. Some people were convinced that if, for instance, you were merely one half of a peasant couple dancing jolly peasant dances on a stage full of other peasant couples, then you might as well forget about having any future with the company. If, on the other hand, you were given a solo…

Both Jen and Sean had been given solos. Jen had danced the Fairy of the Crystal Fountain from *Sleeping Beauty*, Sean had done the Miller's Dance from *Three-Cornered Hat*. They had both gone on to join the company.

"It's all so nerve-racking," sighed Caitlyn. "Don't you find it so? Maddy?" She nudged me. "Don't you find it nerve-racking?"

I said, "What? Oh! Yes." I came to with a start. I'd

been so bound up in thoughts of my audition – it was already becoming *my audition* – that I really hadn't been paying proper attention. "It's nerve-racking," I said.

She looked at me, reproachfully. "You're just saying that to make me feel better. You obviously don't find it nerve-racking at all!"

I assured her that I did. "I think we all do – even Tiffany."

I am not at all a worrying kind of person. I tend to do what Dad calls *taking things in my stride*. (What Mum sometimes calls *being complacent*.) But even I felt a few tremors when I was actually forced to stop and think about it. Imagining how it would be having to watch while others – Tiffany, for example – got to dance solos and you were relegated to a measly minor role as a Snowflake or a stupid clumping peasant. It wouldn't just be a question of hurt pride; it would be all your hopes and dreams crashing to the ground. It was generally accepted as fact that no one who had been passed over for *Showtime* ever made it into the company. Or, for that matter, ever made a name for themselves as a dancer anywhere. I wasn't sure how I would be able to deal with that. Maybe sometime, one day, when I was older, I might want to turn to acting, but not because I'd failed as a dancer! Because I was *good* at it. If I really was good at it. If I—

"You must admit it's frightening," wailed Caitlyn. "Our whole futures could be at stake!"

"I know," I said. "I know."

If I did take an audition, I could maybe do the balcony scene from *Romeo and Juliet*. I already knew it practically off by heart, and Steph had said they were working on the play, so that would make it a good choice. If there was just some way I could arrange it without Mum finding out!

"It's not so much frightening," said Caitlyn, "as absolutely terrifying!"

"Just stop dwelling," I said. "We'll find out soon enough."

"D'you think so? When do you think they'll put the lists up?"

"Soon," I said.

"But it's already gone half-term!"

Half-term, I thought. *That would have been a good time to have an audition.*

"I mean, how long will they give us to I—"

"I don't know!"

If I had only thought to set it up for half-term, it would have solved all my problems. I could have told Mum I was meeting Caitlyn and gone off to have the audition without Mum ever needing to know.

"Couldn't you ask Sean?"

I frowned. "Ask him what?"

"When they tell people what they're going to be doing!"

"He wouldn't remember. It was ages ago for him. If you're that bothered," I said, "why not ask Mrs Elkins?"

She shrank back, immediately. "I couldn't do that!"

"Well, then," I said, "you'll just have to wait patiently, like the rest of us."

I had told Caitlyn not to dwell; I wasn't going to,

either. The chances were Ms Hickman had already finalised the programme for *Showtime*. She almost certainly knew who was going to be dancing what, so there wasn't anything to be gained from agonising over it. There was nothing I could do. But I *could* do something about my audition!

The main problem was how to go about arranging it without Mum finding out. Suppose I just rang them up and asked, please could I have an audition? Would they let me? Without talking to Mum or Dad? And suppose they said yes and then sent a letter giving me details, like time and date and how many audition pieces I needed to prepare? And then suppose the envelope had *Rosemount Stage School* printed on it, like City Ballet School printed their name on things, and Mum got to the post before I did? Which she almost certainly would, unless it arrived on a Saturday, when classes didn't start so early. Even then, Mum was usually up before me.

It was all so difficult! There was only one solution: I would just have to go back to Layton Road and call in in person. *Without Caitlyn*. It was just a question of how and when.

And then on Saturday I got the opportunity. Word was going round the school that a very famous dancer from the Royal Danish Ballet, Christen Jensen, who was guesting with the company for the season, was actually in the building *right now* and was rehearsing with Toni Bergman, one of the company's leading soloists.

"I saw them!" panted Roz. "I had a peep through the windows and I saw them!"

"They must have been there all morning," said Chloe. "They'll have to break soon."

It was generally agreed that we couldn't all gather like a load of gawkers outside the studio and lie in wait, that would be a bit *too* naff, and in any case would get us into deep trouble if a member of staff caught us at it. What we *could* do, said Alex, was go up to the refectory and wait there, in the hope that after such a long rehearsal they would decide to snatch a bite to eat.

"They're bound to be starving!"

"That," said Amber, "is a really neat idea. Who's coming?"

Everyone, it seemed – except me.

"You don't want to stay and see them?" cried Roz.

I wasn't that bothered about seeing Toni cos she was in and out of the building all the time. I would rather have liked to see Christen. If I was ever going to have a crush on anyone it would be him! When I was little, like about nine or ten, I used to have these fantasies that I was dancing Clara in *The Nutcracker* and Christen was my Prince. For a moment I was torn, but very firmly I reminded myself that this was my chance to go back to Rosemount without Caitlyn tagging along and getting all worried and suspicious, so I excused myself by saying that I'd promised Mum I'd be home in time for lunch.

I didn't feel in the least guilty as I walked up Layton Road and through the doors of Rosemount. It was *just an audition*. Nothing more.

The doors opened on to a foyer, with photos of what I assumed were former pupils covering the walls. I'd have liked to linger and look and see if there was anyone I'd heard of, but a woman was standing there, at a reception desk, sorting papers. She was very tall and elegant, with a mass of jet-black hair piled dramatically on top of her head.

"Hallo!" She smiled at me, encouragingly. "How can I help you?"

"Are you Mrs Ashworth?" I said.

She nodded. "I am! What can I do for you?"

"I'd like to arrange for an audition," I said.

"Oh." She looked a bit surprised. Perhaps she wasn't used to people just walking in and demanding auditions. "All right, let's see what we can do. Were you thinking of coming to us full-time or part-time?

I frowned. "What would be the difference?"

"Well, if you wanted to come as a full-time student you would have to wait until the next academic year before you started, whereas if you wanted to enrol part-time you could come more or less straight away."

"But would it be the same audition?"

"Similar, though we do require rather more from our full-time applicants. It's not that we don't demand high standards from all of our students, but obviously if you're only here part-time it means you do have other demands made on you, whereas we expect our full-time students to be committed one hundred per cent."

That decided me: it was full-time or nothing! The part-time audition was obviously rubbish. Like the difference between auditioning for Babette's Babes and auditioning for City Ballet School. Babette's Babes would take just about anyone that could kick their legs high enough and keep in time to the music. I wanted to know whether I'd be considered good enough to join Steph and the others full-time. Not, of course, that I *would* be joining them. But I still wanted to know!

"When could I come and do it?" I said.

"Well, first of all you'll need to fill in one of our application forms and get your mum or dad to sign it for you."

"I can do that," I said.

"All right. Well, here you are, let me give you one."
She opened a drawer and took out a sheet of paper.
"Bring this back and then we can arrange a date."

I hesitated. "Could we arrange the date now?"

"Now?" She seemed amused. "I suppose we could,
if you're that desperate."

"I am!" I said. "I want to do it as soon as I possibly
can."

"So what shall we say? Is a Saturday morning good
for you?"

"Next Saturday?" I said, hopefully.

"Oh, dear me, no!" She laughed. "Not that quickly,
I'm afraid. Let me have a look on the computer and see
what we've got. How about… Saturday week? That's
the earliest we could possibly fit you in. Could you
manage Saturday week?"

I nodded, eagerly. I could manage whatever she
wanted!

"Could you make it early? Say, nine o'clock?"

"That would be brilliant," I said.

"You'll find all the details on the form. You'll need to prepare a speech and have a song ready, or you can dance, if you prefer. But do you really think you're giving yourself enough time?"

I said, "Yes! I've been practising."

"Let me make a note… nine o'clock, Saturday week. You haven't told me your name?"

"Oh," I said. "It's –" I hesitated. "It's Jordan! Jordan Barker."

Jordan had been one of my two best friends at school, before I left for CBS. I hadn't been planning on pretending to be her! I hadn't planned on pretending to be anyone. It just suddenly seemed safer not to tell my real name in case Mrs Ashworth guessed who I was.

Oh! You must be Sean O'Brien's sister!

It did sometimes make life difficult, having not only a brother but an entire family who were famous. Famous in the ballet world, that is. It meant that I could never just be *me*. Maddy O'Brien in her own right. But if Dad knew about Rosemount it was quite likely that Mrs Ashworth knew about my family, especially as Mum's ballet school was not a million miles away. Some of the kids at Rosemount might even have had classes there! And of course Steph and the others, and probably Mrs Ashworth, as well, had been at that performance of *Romeo*, when Steph had recognised me. I just hoped I didn't bump into her on the way out. It would ruin all my plans if she gave the game away by calling after me.

Mrs Ashworth said, "All right, then, Jordan, I'll see you on Saturday week. And you'll make sure to get the form signed and send it back to me?"

"Absolutely," I said. "I'm going to do it straight away!" And then, at the door, I hesitated. "There is just one thing…"

"What's that?"

"How long will it be before I know if I've passed the audition?"

"That would depend which audition you were planning to take, full-time or part-time."

I said, "Full-time! Will you be able to tell me immediately?"

She laughed again. "You really are keen, aren't you?"

"I am!" I said.

"Well, I'm sorry to disappoint you but you may have to wait a little while. It's rarely as simple as a straightforward yes or no. There are so many factors to take into account. Sometimes we have to put people on a waiting list, for instance. It really depends how many places we have available."

I said, "Oh."

"Try not to look so downcast! I promise we'll let you know as soon as possible. You can normally expect a letter about two to three weeks after the audition. Don't worry about it, just get your form filled in. That's the first step."

"I'm going home to do it right now," I said. I couldn't wait!

Chapter Seven

It took me ages to fill in the audition form. It was a bit more complicated than I'd expected. I'd thought it would just be a question of ticking boxes and then putting a signature at the end, but they wanted to know if I'd had any acting or stage experience and where I went to school. I had to keep thinking about what to put. I didn't want to say I'd done ballet, just in case, so I left that part blank. And I knew I couldn't say I was at City Ballet School, so after a bit of dithering I wrote "Coombe House", which was where I'd gone before. I didn't see that it mattered; it wasn't as if anyone was going to check. Not unless they offered me a place, and even if they did I wouldn't be able to accept it, so why would they bother? And anyway, it wasn't like I was giving false information. Not properly false. I mean, it wasn't a *lie*. Exactly. I *had* been at Coombe House. For years and years!

It did feel a bit strange saying that I was Jordan Barker. And I did have a little twinge of conscience when I signed the form as her mum: *Marion Barker*, in what I hoped was suitably grown-up writing.

Just for a minute I had a few doubts and wondered if what I was doing was illegal. Forgery is a criminal offence! Except that I wasn't really forging, was I? It wasn't as if I was trying to make it look like Jordan's mum's real signature. I'd never even seen her real signature! All I was doing was just writing her name on a form. There's no law against writing someone's name; not as far as I know. It wasn't like I was trying to steal money, or anything. I just wanted to have my audition!

All the same, I couldn't help the uncomfortable feeling that I might be committing some kind of offence. Even if it wasn't actually a crime to write the name Marion Barker and pretend she was my mum, it might still be breaking some law or other.

For a moment I was almost tempted to go downstairs and throw myself on Mum's mercy. Explain how I really, really, *really* wanted to prove that I could act. How I'd always wanted to act, ever since I could remember. Dance, too, of course; that went without saying. You couldn't be Mum and Dad's daughter and not want to dance! But what could be the harm in just having an audition? *Please*, Mum. *Please!*

I knew what Mum would say. She would say, *For goodness' sake, Maddy!* And then she would lecture me about how training to be a dancer was a full-time commitment.

You either do it wholeheartedly or you don't do it at all!

It's what she'd once said to me years ago when I begged to be let off a Saturday morning class so I could go shopping with my friends. Out of the question!

Dad might be a little more sympathetic, but even he

would probably tell me to just concentrate on one thing at a time. Either that or he would say, *Ask your mum.* He can be such a coward!

I couldn't even pour out my feelings to Sean. I'd tried that last term, when I'd been so eager to prove I could ice skate. He'd warned me not to, and I'd gone against his advice and nearly got thrown out as a result.

Was I crazy, putting myself at risk all over again?

Caitlyn would say that I was, but Caitlyn is a natural-born worrier. I think in life you have to seize every opportunity. Go for it, is my motto! I don't see that you can ever hope to get anywhere if you're not prepared to take the occasional risk, though really what possible risk could there be in just having one little secret audition that no one would ever know about?

Boldly, I filled in Jordan's address. There! It was done. I folded the form and slipped it down the side of my school bag. All I had to do was ring Jordan and tell her what I was up to. I was glad that I'd picked on Jordan rather than Livi, who was my other best friend at

Coombe. Livi's mum and dad are rather high-powered and important sort of people, whereas Jordan's are more comfortable and ordinary. Even if Jordan's mum was somehow to discover what I'd done she would be more likely to understand and be sympathetic. She'd once said to Jordan that she thought it must be difficult for me, having a family that was so single-minded.

I rang Jordan straight away. She grew very excited when I told her what I'd done.

"Ooh," she squealed, "a conspiracy!"

"I just don't want to upset Mum," I told her. "If she knew, she'd get all worried and think I didn't want to be a dancer any more."

"But you do?" urged Jordan, suddenly sounding a bit anxious.

I reassured her that of course I did.

"Cos I mean, it's who you are," said Jordan. "You've always been going to be a dancer! Ever since I've known you. Dancing –" she said it very solemnly – "is your destiny."

I thought, *People don't always have to fulfil their destinies.* There was such a thing as free will. In other words, *choice.* It seemed to me that I had never really been given much in the way of choice. It had just been assumed from the very beginning that I was going to dance. Which I probably still would, but it had to be my decision!

"This isn't to do with me being a dancer," I told Jordan. "It's about finding out whether I can act."

But everybody knows you can," said Jordan. "Don't you remember that term we did scenes from *Alice in Wonderland* and you were Alice and the local paper had a picture of you and everyone said how good you were?"

"That was when I was *seven,*" I said. "And Liv played the Queen of Hearts and everybody said how good *she* was."

"She didn't have her picture in the paper!"

"Only cos her mum wasn't a famous dancer."

"I used to envy you, having a famous family," said Jordan. "I'm not so sure, now. Not if it means having to have conspiracies. What d'you think your mum'd say if she found out?"

"She'd go ballistic," I said. "That's why she mustn't ever know."

"What happens if they offer you a place?"

"I suppose…" I said it reluctantly. "I suppose I'd have to turn it down."

"You mean you would actually *want* to go, If you could?"

"What I'd really like," I said, eagerly, "is to do both."

"Acting *and* dancing?"

"Yes!" The thought was exciting. "But obviously –" I sighed. "Obviously I can't. Not until I'm loads older. Maybe when I have to retire from ballet I could become an actress. Lots of dancers do. But that's why I need to know for sure that I'm any good!"

I was haunted by all the totally untalented little darlings that turned up at Mum's studio cos their mums or their grans had said what wonderful dancers they were when in reality, as Mum didn't hesitate to point out, they had no hope at all of ever getting anywhere. I didn't want to be a totally untalented little darling thinking I could act just cos my friends assured me that I could!

"So, OK," said Jordan. "Let me make sure I understand. They're going to send me a letter—"

"They're going to send *me* a letter," I corrected her, very firmly. "But it'll be addressed to you cos that's who I told them I was."

"You told them that you're me." Jordan sounded entranced by the idea. Someone pretending to be her!

"Is that all right?" I said.

"It's never happened before," said Jordan. "No one's ever wanted to be me!"

It would have seemed unkind to point out that I could just as easily have picked Livi, instead. It had been pure chance that had made me use Jordan's name.

"What do you want me to do," she said, "when I've got it? This letter. Do you want me to read it and tell you what it says?"

I said, "No, I just want you to ring me and tell me it's come."

"And then open it?"

I said, "No!" I didn't want Jordan reading my letter before I did. "Send it to me. In a different envelope!"

"Oh. Yes! Of course. To stop your mum seeing who it's from."

"Exactly." I nodded. "You could even write your name on the back so she'll know it's just you."

Jordan giggled again. "This is fun! It's like being in a spy movie."

"It's very important to me," I said.

"So when do you think it'll come?"

"Well, I'm having the audition the Saturday after next, so maybe... about... two weeks after that?"

"I'll watch out for it," promised Jordan.

"There is just one thing," I said. "They might address it to your mum."

"To my *mum*?"

"Cos I had to put her name on the form... on account of me being you."

"Oh. Right! The plot thickens." Jordan was obviously

enjoying herself. It really was just as well, I thought, that I'd chosen her and not Liv. Liv is far more serious-minded. She might have raised annoying objections, like telling me that identity theft was a crime, or she didn't think it right to aid and abet me. Jordan was just eager to aid and abet in any way she could.

"It might be awkward," I said, "if it's got your mum's name on it."

"Oh, you don't have to worry about Mum," said Jordan. "I'll think of something to tell her." She suddenly went off into a renewed peal of giggles. "I could tell her I thought maybe *I* could audition for drama school!"

"What, and you think she'd believe you?"

"Don't see why not," said Jordan.

I didn't remind her of what had happened when we did our scenes from *Alice*, all those years ago. Jordan had been cast as the Dormouse, and had been so overcome by embarrassment that she'd disappeared under the table, taking the tablecloth and all the cups and saucers with her, and had refused to come out.

"Well, or maybe," she said, obviously having second thoughts, "I'll just make sure I get to the post before anyone else does. Dad always leaves really early, and if Mum's on nights she'll probably have gone straight up to bed and be asleep already. No problem!"

It was a weight off my mind. Now I just had to prepare for the audition…

I'd spent a long time wondering what song I should sing. I'd finally decided on "Me and My Mates" from *Polly*. I didn't mind doing the same musical as Steph had done but I didn't want to do the exact same number, it would have seemed too much like copying. In any case, I reckoned that "Me and my Mates" was more my sort of thing. It's sung by Polly herself and is a bit cheeky, whereas "If I Had Three Wishes", which was what Steph had chosen, was more romantic.

In spite of not being a singer I knew that I had an OK sort of voice and could keep in tune, but I also knew that I would need to put in lots of practice, which meant spending ages locked away in my bedroom, listening on YouTube and then singing in front of the long mirror on the inside of my wardrobe door. The big problem was that if Mum or Dad were at home I didn't dare sing too loudly in case they wondered what I was up to and came to investigate. It would be easy enough to invent some story, but I felt I'd probably done enough inventing for the time being. I'd already invented a new name for myself, and a new mum. Even if it didn't exactly make me feel guilty, I still had these little moments of doubt, wondering if it was something that could get me into trouble. Big trouble! *Again.*

I was downstairs one afternoon, singing full pelt cos of Mum and Dad both being out, when Sean and Danny suddenly appeared without any warning. I hadn't even realised they were there until I reached the end of the song and they both started applauding.

I beamed. I couldn't help it! Eagerly I said, "So what do you think?"

Sean said, "Well, you certainly have a very loud voice... we could hear you halfway down the road!"

"But is it *tuneful*?" I said.

"It's loud," said Sean. "Talk about GBH of the eardrums!"

"What's that s'posed to mean?"

"Grievous bodily harm?" said Sean.

"To your *eardrums*?"

"Seriously, just take it down a notch. What's it in aid of, anyway?"

"Not in aid of anything," I said. "I was just singing. That's all."

"And doing it very nicely," Danny assured me.

"And all without a mike," marvelled Sean.

"Well, at least she could make herself heard in the back row of the stalls."

"But isn't that good?" I said.

"Good if you're in the back row of the stalls," agreed Sean. "Might need earplugs if you were at the front."

"Stop teasing her," said Danny.

"So, seriously," said Sean, "what's brought all this on? You're not planning a career in musicals, are you?"

I said, *"No!"*

I must have said it a bit too vehemently cos Sean's eyes narrowed, almost like he suspected something. But how could he? He couldn't! No way.

"Don't take any notice of him," said Danny. "He's probably just jealous because one of you can sing in tune."

But we both could! I looked at Sean, doubtfully. Was I really too loud? Loud meant raucous. It meant people clapping their hands over their ears. Maybe I should have chosen a different song, like the one Steph had sung. Something softer. More lyrical. Now I didn't know what to do! Danny had said my voice was tuneful, but what did he know? He wasn't a singer!

Well, but neither was Sean, so what did he know, if it came to that? I couldn't keep chopping and changing! It was far too late. My audition was only a few days away.

For the first time, I began to feel a bit nervous. I'd trained for years and years before taking the audition for City Ballet School. I hadn't trained *at all* for this one. I hadn't even had anyone help me prepare. I'd had to do it all myself! And then when I turned to Sean, hoping for a bit of brotherly encouragement, all he could think to say was that my voice was too loud.

Danny was right; I shouldn't take any notice of him! A loud voice didn't necessarily mean raucous. A loud voice was a BIG voice – which was a hundred times better than a little tiny thin one that nobody could hear.

That decided me. There simply wasn't any point in worrying. I could only give it my best shot, as Dad would say.

Chapter Eight

I had to leave home at practically crack of dawn on Saturday. Well, half-past seven, which is a time when I am normally still asleep and being yelled at to "Get up! Get up *now*!"

Mum was amazed when she came into the kitchen and found me already there, spooning yoghurt into my mouth. She wanted to know what I was doing out of bed so early. I pulled a face and said, "They've gone and squeezed in an extra class." *More* invention. It seems once you start it's never-ending. You invent one thing and it immediately leads to another.

Mum said, "Wait until you start rehearsing for your end-of-term show… They'll be squeezing in extra classes all day long! I suppose you haven't heard anything yet? You don't know what you'll be doing?"

I said, "Nope. Not yet."

"Well, let me know as soon as you hear. I hope they give you something worthwhile. I'm sure they will!"

I promised I would tell Mum the minute I knew anything and went whizzing up the road to the Underground. Our first class on a Saturday didn't actually start till ten o'clock, so I reckoned I should be all right. Even if the audition went on for half an hour, which I didn't think it would, that still gave me time to get the Tube to Waterloo and hurry down the Cut to school. Nobody need ever know where I had been. Not even Caitlyn!

I found that I was quite nervous as I approached Rosemount. I'm not used to feeling nervous! Even when we'd had our audition for City Ballet School and everyone around me was quivering and quaking, I'd remained perfectly calm. I always do. Some people accuse me of being insensitive, or even big-headed – *I'm*

Madeleine O'Brien! I can't fail! But it wasn't either of those. I *never* think "I'm Madeleine O'Brien" like it makes me someone special. And I'm not insensitive! I can understand why Caitlyn, for instance, sometimes doubts herself. It's just that when you've been bullied and browbeaten by your own mum since you were three years old you tend to know whether or not you're any good. Mum *does* bully and browbeat, but she is an excellent teacher and I trust her judgement absolutely. I just wished I'd had a teacher to help me with my Rosemount audition, especially with the song. "Me and my Mates" was quite a bouncy sort of number and I'd even worked out some little movements to go with it. Funny ones! The top notes weren't too high, and I knew that I could keep in tune, but being able to keep in tune doesn't necessarily mean that you can sing, any more than being able to do the splits, for instance, means that you can dance, even though there are some misguided people who think that it does.

I was glad, at any rate, that I was having my audition

so early, before classes began and everyone started to arrive. It would have made me feel inferior, being surrounded by people who had already taken their auditions and been accepted. People who *knew* they could act. Or sing. I really wasn't confident at all about my singing, especially after what Sean had said. If I sang full out they might complain of grievous bodily harm; but singing quietly is a whole lot more difficult. At least, it seemed to me that it was. Maybe that was just because I wasn't a trained singer. Maybe I should have done some dancing, instead. But then if they were to offer me a place I wouldn't know whether it was because they were impressed by my acting or just by my dancing. Anyway, it was too late now. Mrs Ashworth had come smiling out to greet me.

"Jordan," she said. "Good girl! Nice and early!" But even as she spoke I saw her eyes flicker towards the door, as if she were expecting someone else to appear. "All by yourself?" she said. "No mum or dad?"

Quickly I said that Dad was away and Mum couldn't

get time off work. Yet more invention! I hadn't realised I was supposed to bring a parent with me.

"Well, never mind." Mrs Ashworth opened a door marked AUDITORIUM and ushered me through. "I take it you have your application form? All properly filled in?"

"*And* signed," I said, giving it to her.

"Excellent! All right, then, Jordan, up you go." She gestured towards a small stage with a piano on it. "This is my assistant Mr Burns, by the way. He'll provide you with any accompaniment you need. So! What are you proposing to do for us?"

I bounced up on to the stage. "**I'M GOING TO—**"

I stopped. I was shouting! What was I shouting for? I cleared my throat and tried again.

"I'm going to do Juliet's balcony speech from *Romeo and Juliet*, a play by William Shakespeare, and 'Me and My Mates' from *Polly*, a musical by—"

I stopped again. Who was it by? I didn't know!

"Arnold Gold?" suggested Mrs Ashworth, kindly.

"Yes!" I beamed, trying to make like I'd known it all along. "Arnold Gold."

"And which will you be giving us first?"

"Um... the song?"

"Whichever you choose. It's up to you."

"So the song," I said. I really wanted to have it over and done, so I could get on to the Shakespeare.

"You've brought the music with you, I hope?"

I said, "M-music?" My heart sank. I hadn't realised I was supposed to bring the music!

"No? Well, never mind," said Mrs Ashworth. "I'm sure we can help out. Mr Burns –" she turned to the man sitting next to her – "Do we have it anywhere, do you suppose?"

"We do." Mr Burns came up on to the stage and seated himself at the piano. "We have it right here... if I can just lay my hands on it." He began leafing through a pile of sheet music on top of the piano. "Here we go! Which song are you going to give us? 'Me and my Mates'? Got it! Problem solved. All right? Ready when you are."

I tried my best not to cause grievous bodily harm but I think I must have sung quite loud cos at the end Mrs Ashworth said, "Well, it makes a change, does it not –" she turned to Mr Burns – "to find someone who's not afraid to open up?"

Mr Burns smiled and said, "It does indeed."

They didn't make it sound like opening up was a *bad* thing, and I hadn't noticed either of them wincing or clamping their hands to their ears, so maybe Sean simply didn't have any idea what he was talking about. It wouldn't be the first time! It was a family joke that before I was born Mum had shown him a picture of me when I was still inside her and he'd thought it was a picture of a bean... admittedly he was only a few years old, but even at a few years old you'd think you'd know better than to imagine people had *beans* growing inside them. One thing I knew for sure, he wasn't any kind of expert on singing.

But anyway, I'd got through it and now, at last, I could do my Juliet speech. The really important part of the audition!

There were two chairs standing at the back of the stage. I dragged them down to the front and placed them side by side, facing inwards so that I could kneel on them and pretend they were a balcony.

"*Romeo and Juliet,*" I announced. "Act II, Scene 2. It is night time and Juliet is standing on her balcony, staring into the garden and dreaming of Romeo."

I'd taken great care, writing the introduction. I was quite proud of it! No one had actually told me that you had to set the scene; to explain where it took place, and when, and which part I was playing. I'd worked it out for myself. I couldn't expect everyone to be as familiar with the play as I was.

I made sure not to cause any grievous bodily harm with my Juliet speech. It seemed to me that Juliet wouldn't dare speak too loudly in case someone heard her. Lady Capulet, maybe, or the old fat Nurse. She would be in deep trouble if they discovered she was out there, on the balcony, hoping to see Romeo. At the same time, of course, I knew I had to speak loudly enough for the audience to hear me – that is, Mrs Ashworth and Mr Burns. They obviously did cos when I'd finished Mrs Ashworth said, "Thank you so much, Jordan. I really enjoyed that! And thank you also for coming in today. We'll be in touch just as soon as we can."

I flew back up the road as if on wings. Part of me was exultant! I had experienced exactly the same thrill, the same excitement, as if I had just given an actual performance. Which of course, in some ways, I had. It might only have been one short speech, but I had stood up in front of real professional acting people and put everything I could into it. *Thank you so much, Jordan. I really enjoyed that!*

Unfortunately, if one part of me was exultant another was starting to panic. I had just seen the time! If I didn't go like the wind I would be late for class. They are very strict about timekeeping at CBS. If you're even just a few minutes late it's a black mark.

Of course, on this morning of all mornings the train

had to crawl. And then come to a complete *stop* between stations. Really frustrating! By the time it finally heaved itself into Waterloo I could tell that I was never going to make it for ten o'clock.

I tore down the Cut like I was supercharged, hurled myself through the doors of CBS and hurtled downstairs to the girls' changing room just as the hands on the big clock in the entrance hall were clicking on to the hour. Fortunately I'd come prepared for an emergency and had put on my tights and leotard before leaving home, so it was only my shoes I had to bother with. Fortunately also, our first class was always taken by Mrs Elkins, who is more forgiving than Madam, say, or Ms Hickman, both of whom can be quite scary. Well, Madam can be scary. Ms Hickman can be downright mean!

I shot through the studio door at precisely five minutes past ten. I knew it was five minutes past ten cos that was what the big clock had said as I whizzed back past it, up the stairs. Five minutes is nothing! Class probably wouldn't even have got started.

But it had. Everyone was at the barre and Mrs Rose, at the piano, was dutifully plonking. Even then, had it been Mrs Elkins she would probably just have frowned and waved me into place. Instead, I found myself confronted with the dread figure of Ms Hickman, face contorted, lips pursed into a thin line. Frigidly she said, "Well, Madeleine? And what time do you call this?"

I didn't get the feeling she actually wanted me to tell her that it was five minutes past ten so I muttered that I was really, really sorry.

"There was a hold-up on the Tube."

"Indeed?" said Ms Hickman. You could practically see the frost forming in the air as she spoke. Why did I have the feeling she didn't think I was telling the truth? I *was* telling the truth! There *had* been a hold-up.

"Refresh my memory," said Ms Hickman. "How long, now, have you been travelling in to school on the Underground?"

I said, "Um... a year?"

"And you don't think that after all this time you should

be aware that Tube trains cannot infrequently be held up?"

I swallowed. "It got stuck," I mumbled. "Outside the station."

"An event which you have never known to happen before?"

There was a silence while she coldly awaited my answer. Except that I couldn't think of one!

I was aware of everybody looking at me. Sympathetically, for the most part, though Tiffany was probably enjoying it. She loves it when anyone gets into trouble. But Caitlyn shot me a concerned glance, and Nico, behind Ms Hickman's back, pulled a funny face by way of encouragement.

"Well? I'm waiting," said Ms Hickman.

I muttered again that I was very sorry.

"Sorry is not good enough," she snapped. "I have to ask myself, Madeleine, whether you really want to be here?"

"I do!" I said.

"In that case, may I suggest that in future you leave home half an hour earlier and arrive here when you are supposed to arrive? I really cannot, and will not, tolerate any more of this careless attitude towards your work! Apart from anything else, it betrays a selfishness, which is totally unacceptable. You have interrupted us all and wasted not only my time but everybody else's. Now, take your place at the barre –" I slipped in, quickly, behind Roz – "and attempt, if you will, to fade into the background. If you don't think you can manage to do that, then I suggest you absent yourself. Which is it to be?"

Meekly I said that I would fade into the background.

"Horrible old witch," muttered Roz.

First thing Monday, the cast lists went up for the end-of-term show. It was Amber who alerted us. She fell panting into the changing room, gibbering like some kind of mad person.

"They're here! They're here!"

"Omigod, are we in danger?" said Roz.

"*What?*" Amber stared at her, wildly. "What are you talking about?"

"What are *you* talking about?" said Chloe.

"The lists! The cast lists! They're here! In the hall! Come, quickly!"

Amber went racing off down the corridor, hotly pursued by the rest of us in various states of undress. Mei was hopping with one shoe on and one shoe off, Alex didn't have any shoes at all. Even the great Tiffany was still struggling to pin her hair into its regulation bun.

We tumbled down the stairs and spilled into the hall in a breathless gaggle.

"There!"

Amber pointed with a quivering finger at the noticeboard on the back wall. We gathered, nervously, in front of it, aware that what we were about to learn might foretell our entire future.

"OK, guys!" Tiffany plunged forward. "The moment of truth!"

I'll say one thing for Tiffany, she has what it takes.

But so do I! I am a firm believer in what Mum calls *facing up*. I pushed past all the ditherers and inserted myself next to Tiffany. Immediately all the rest of them started jostling and shoving, trying to peer over our shoulders.

"I can't see! I can't see!"

"What does it say?"

"Casts for Summer Show..."

"But who's got what?"

"Third year—"

"Never mind third year! What about us?"

Quickly, I ran my eye down the list:

Caitlyn Hughes, Oliver Merchant ... *Spectre de la Rose.*

Tiffany Blanche, Jonathan Finch ... *ZigZag, 2nd variation*

Mei Wong, Christopher Islip ... *Lovers' Meeting, pas de deux*

Rosalie Costello, Pieter van Dieren ... *Couples at a Ball, 1st couple*

★ 143 ☆

Amber ......, Lucas Whibley .... *Couples at a*
Ball, 2nd couple

Alexandra Ellman, Mischa .... *Bombe*
Surprise

All around me there came little squeaks and grunts as
people discovered their fate. Tiffany went "*Wow!*" and
punched the air. Mei gave a little joyous squeal. Someone
– I wasn't sure who – let out a long, quivering sigh. I
stood, silently, in the midst of it all, my heart hammering.
Where was *my* name? What was *I* going to be doing? I
had to do something!

Nobody but me seemed to have noticed that I hadn't
been included. And then, suddenly, Chloe cried,
"Where's Maddy? Why isn't Maddy there?"

"*Maddy!*"

They all spun round to look at me. Caitlyn said,
"Maddy?"

I shook my head. No use asking me. It was Ms
Hickman who had the final word on casting. How could

I be expected to know what went on in her warped mind?

"It has to be a mistake," said Roz.

Unless – oh, God! – she had somehow discovered what I had been up to? But how could she? There was no way!

It was exactly what I'd thought when I'd gone ice skating. *How could she know? Who could have told her?* In that instance it had been Amber – though I don't *think* she did it on purpose. But Amber had only known about the ice skating cos she'd turned out to be friends with Sonya, the girl who'd invited me. She surely couldn't be friends with Mrs Ashworth? Even if she was, Mrs Ashworth didn't know that I was Madeleine O'Brien. She thought I was Jordan!

It did nothing to answer the question: *where was my name?* Nico's, too, come to that. Was he being punished as well as me?

Tides of guilt and remorse came flooding over me. Nico would never forgive me! And however would I tell Mum? She would be so angry! So would Dad. Not even Jen would have any sympathy. Not even Sean. When I'd thought, last year, that I was going to be thrown out he'd let me cry all over him and done his best to comfort me. This time I'd be on my own. No shoulder to cry on. No words of comfort. I'd brought it all on myself!

Caitlyn was looking at me, distressed. Urgently she whispered, "Maddy! What have you done?"

Nothing! I'd done nothing! Just taken an audition; that was all. What was so wrong about taking an audition? And why did Caitlyn automatically assume I'd done anything, anyway?

Suddenly, from somewhere behind us, we heard Mrs Elkins' voice.

"Make way, girls! Let me come through. Maddy, I must apologise." She waved a sheet of paper in the air. "Page two! Somehow or other, it got left behind. I hope you're not panicking? No need! You haven't been forgotten."

She pinned the sheet of paper below the first one and turned to go. Immediately we all clustered back round the board. This time I didn't hesitate to use my elbows and shove people out of the way.

"Oh!" I clapped a hand to my mouth. I could hardly believe what I was seeing! But there it was, in front of me, in black and white:

Madeleine O'Brien, Nicholas Porter ... *balcony* *scene, Romeo and Juliet*

The balcony scene! My special scene! The one I'd worked so hard on!

Chloe said, "Well, was that worth waiting for or was that worth waiting for?"

I felt a huge beam spread across my face. I'd dreamt of being Juliet ever since we'd done the play. Even before we'd done the play. Long, long before! I suddenly had this memory of being taken to a performance of the ballet when I was still quite little and re-enacting the balcony scene in my bedroom afterwards. How romantic it had seemed! To die for love! I had self-importantly informed Mum that "I'm going to dance the part of Juliet when I'm older." I'd always believed that one day I would, but I'd never, ever thought, not even for a moment, that it would be Ms Hickman who entrusted me with the part. Ms Hickman, of all people! Ms Hickman hated me! Well, maybe not hated exactly; but I really didn't think I was one of her favourite people.

I said this to Caitlyn as we made our way home later in the day.

"I honestly thought, after the way she went on at me yesterday, she'd probably gone and told Mrs Elkins I didn't deserve to do *any*thing, let alone Juliet!"

"It's a beautiful *pas de deux*," said Caitlyn.

"It's one of my absolute, all-time favourites! But how about you?" I said. "*Spectre de la Rose!*"

Spectre was one of the most famous ballets from the time of the great Russian impresario Diaghilev, originally danced by Nijinsky and Karsavina. With new choreography by Dad it had only come back into the company repertoire earlier in the year, so really, I thought, Caitlyn ought to feel truly honoured. Although it was only short – about ten minutes – the ballet critic Dominic Brand had described it as a "miniature masterpiece".

It was everything she loved best: romantic music, romantic storyline. Not that there was very much of a story. Simply a young girl, asleep in the moonlight, dreaming of the handsome young man she's just met at the ball. She's still clutching the red rose that he's given her. And then, as she sighs in her sleep, the young man – the spirit of the rose – suddenly appears at her bedroom window. The young girl wakes up, the young man leaps gracefully into the room, and they dance a very beautiful – and *very romantic* – *pas de deux*, at the end of which the young man disappears as suddenly as he came, leaving the young girl dancing on her own in the moonlight, happily smiling as she presses the rose to her lips.

It sounds kind of soppy written down, but it is just about one of *the* most romantic ballets Dad has ever done, as different as could be from the athletic contortions of *ZigZag*. Audiences love it! And Caitlyn couldn't have been a better choice. I suddenly felt moved to give her a quick hug.

"I'm so happy for you!" I said.

"I'm happy for you," said Caitlyn. "I mean, *Juliet*… you must be pleased! You *are* pleased, aren't you?"

She glanced at me, as if not quite certain.

I said, "I'm absolutely thrilled!" I still couldn't quite take it in. *Juliet!*

"It's your part," said Caitlyn. "You've made it your part! Right from when you read it in class. You're going to be absolutely brilliant!"

It takes a lot to embarrass me, but I did go a bit pink at that. Quickly I said, "I bet Tiffany's chuffed! *ZigZag's* right up her street."

"Yes, and Mei and Chris… *Lovers' Meeting*. They'll be really sweet in that."

"We've all done well," I said. "I can't see anyone has much reason to complain."

It was true that First and Second Couples in *Couples at a Ball* weren't the most exciting roles, but at least they weren't stupid peasant dances! And Alex, I thought, had to be happy with *Bombe Surprise*. It might be what Mum called "just a silly bauble" but nobody could deny it was enormous fun.

"See?" I nudged at Caitlyn. "It's what I said right at the beginning... we're obviously a very talented group!"

"I told you not to say that," wailed Caitlyn.

"Yes, cos you reckoned it was tempting fate! So, OK, I tempted it, and look what it's led to... me being Juliet and you doing Dad's latest ballet! Which for your information," I said, "he wouldn't let just anyone dance in. They'd have had to get his permission."

Caitlyn wrinkled her brow. "D'you honestly think so?"

"You'd better believe it! Dad guards his ballets jealously. And think of the shoes you'll be stepping into… Ariana Savalas! She was the one he wrote it for. Her and Sean."

Caitlyn turned a glowing face towards me. "We've both been really lucky," she said, "haven't we?"

If I hadn't been feeling so triumphant I might taken exception to that. It was more than just luck! It was dedication, and sacrifice, and really hard work. I said as much, somewhat reproachfully, to Caitlyn.

"Of course, I know you're right," she said. "I know we *are* dedicated and sometimes it really *is* hard work. But I don't feel I'm making any sort of sacrifice! Do you? Honestly? I mean… how can it be sacrifice when we love what we're doing?"

I said, "Just because you love what you're doing doesn't mean you don't sometimes wonder about doing other things."

I thought she would ask me, what sort of things? But she fell silent for a while, before suddenly bursting out with: "Was it really true what you told Ms Hickman about your train being held up?"

"Yes," I snapped, "it was!" Why did everyone doubt me? The train *had* been held up! "What made you ask?"

"Just wondered," said Caitlyn.

"Well, don't," I said, crossly, "cos it's true!"

Chapter Nine

I couldn't wait to get home and tell Mum the news.

"Guess what? I'm dancing Juliet... the balcony scene!"

"Are you really?" said Mum. She sounded quite excited. It is not like Mum to be excited! She's always very cool. I wouldn't have been at all surprised if she'd taken the opportunity to read me a lecture on the subject of proving myself worthy, like, "This is your big chance, so just be sure you make the most of it." In other words, whatever you do, don't go upsetting anyone!

I'd never dared tell her how at the end of my first year I'd almost got myself thrown out, but rumours had obviously reached her that Ms Hickman had originally been in two minds whether to even offer me a place. I knew Mum had her suspicions cos this one time, after I'd done something to upset her she'd given me this long, cold look and said, "I do trust you're not giving Ms Hickman any reason to regret her decision?" I've no idea how Mum ever got to hear about it, and I don't *think* she actually knew for certain, cos if she had there would have been trouble, but Mum does still have very close connections with people in the company, and of course Dad is their resident choreographer, so not much goes on that doesn't come to their attention.

"It's been one of my dreams to dance Juliet," I told her. "I honestly never thought they'd let me!"

"It shows they have faith in you," said Mum.

Daringly I said, "It's Ms Hickman, isn't it, that has the final say?"

"Well, it's Madam who has the absolute final say, but yes," agreed Mum. "It's Ms Hickman who basically runs the school. She must be pleased with your progress."

There was a bit of a pause, and I wondered again just how much Mum knew. Or suspected.

"What did you get to dance," I said, "when it was your summer show?"

"Oh, I can't remember... too long ago! The Black Swan *pas de deux*, I think it was. How about Caitlyn? What is she doing?"

I said, "*Spectre de la Rose.*"

"Excellent!" Mum nodded. "That bodes well for both of you – which is no more than I would expect. I never put people in for auditions unless I have complete faith in their abilities."

I dropped a little curtsey and said, "Yes, Mum. Thank you, Mum!"

"Don't you be cheeky with me," said Mum. "You'd better just brace yourself, my girl, for a hectic few weeks... You're going to be worked off your feet!"

Mum was right. In addition to normal classes we had lots of special ones slotted into the timetable, both before school and after school, and sometimes even all day Saturday. Just as well, I thought, that I'd arranged my Rosemount audition before all the madness began. As it was, I found myself so frantically busy I really didn't have time to keep worrying about when I would hear and whether I'd have got through.

Nico and I were together every day, being taught our roles in *Romeo and Juliet* by an ex-dancer with the company, Pamela Allan. She was an old lady, now, but she had been a famous Juliet in her time, so we felt very honoured. We also felt worn out! In spite of being old, and hobbling with arthritis, Ms Allan really kept us at it. I couldn't remember ever being worked so hard in my life, not even by Mum at her most demanding. But it was worth it. It was so worth it! Nothing, I felt, could be more satisfying than being able, for once, to devote so much time not simply to mastering the steps and the various lifts but to exploring the characters and their feelings. We were Romeo and Juliet, and we were in love! It was every bit as romantic as I'd always dreamt.

"Know what?" said Nico, as we finished a particularly gruelling session one morning. "I'm so glad I got you as a partner!"

"I'm glad I got *you*," I said.

"Do you mean that?" said Nico. "Or are you just saying it?"

Indignantly I assured him that of course I wasn't just saying it. "I can't imagine having a nicer partner!"

"I bet when you first saw us all," said Nico, "I wasn't the one you'd have chosen."

I crinkled my forehead, trying to remember.

"Go on," he said, "admit it! You'd rather have had Carlo."

"Why C— Oh, you mean because he looks Spanish?" Even though he actually wasn't. "As a matter of fact, if you want to know the truth," I said, "I'd probably have gone for Mischa."

"I knew it!" said Nico.

"No, you didn't, you thought I wanted Carlo! Anyway, I bet *you* wouldn't have chosen *me*." His face grew a bit red at that. "You didn't, did you?" I pounced, triumphantly. "So who would you have picked, if you'd been given the choice?"

"Maybe Tiffany," he muttered.

I said, "*Tiffany?* Why Tiffany?"

"I dunno." He hunched a shoulder, looking a bit ashamed of himself. "Just a stupid guy thing, I suppose."

"You mean cos she's stunning?"

She is, unfortunately, even if I hate having to say it. She has this gorgeous blonde hair and deep green eyes, like a cat's, and legs that go on forever. Her extension is amazing! Though some unkind person did once point out that when she did an arabesque she looked a bit like a stork. It's true that in spite of her enviable physique she is not a particularly graceful dancer. And is *far* from being a graceful person. There are times when she can be downright nasty.

I looked at Nico, reproachfully. "You fancied her," I said. "You actually fancied her!"

He hung his head. "I guess."

"So what did you think when you got me?"

"If you want to know the truth," said Nico, "I was absolutely terrified! I thought you were going to be all grand and self-important and keep telling me what I was doing wrong."

I stared at him in disbelief. "Is that how I came across? All grand and self-important?"

"No, but we all knew who you were, and who your brother is, and your mum and dad and everything. It was kind of scary!"

I said, "You never seemed like you were scared."

He grinned. "It only lasted about five minutes. By the end of our first class I knew we were going to get on OK – and boy, was I ever glad they didn't put me with Tiffany!"

"Me, too," I said. "You're my perfect dream partner!"

"Imagine," said Nico, "if we go through the company together and end up famous like Fonteyn and Nureyev!"

"We'll do it," I said. "We'll make it our goal!"

"Let's kiss on it," said Nico.

So we did; and for just a few minutes my Rosemount audition almost completely faded into the background. Hard to believe that just a couple of weeks ago it had loomed so large in my life. If I'd ever imagined, for one minute, that Ms Hickman might give me the chance of dancing Juliet… but how could I possibly have guessed? She was always so cold and cutting! For all that, she obviously had faith in me. Nico, too! He was my partner: dependent on me, just as I was on him. I vowed then that I wouldn't let him down.

I could feel my cheeks beginning to sizzle. Me, who never blushes! We broke apart, suddenly awkward. Thoughts of Rosemount immediately came rushing back; I wasn't quite ready to banish them entirely. Just because I was deliriously happy didn't mean I no longer cared. I was still keen to know whether I'd passed the audition.

Jordan, on the other hand, could hardly control her impatience. I think because she was part of what she called "the conspiracy" she felt she had a personal interest. She rang me three days running just to inform me that the letter hadn't come yet.

"It's too soon," I said.

"So when d'you think it'll get here?"

"Mm… next week, maybe?"

"I'll watch out for it," promised Jordan. "I'll let you know the minute it arrives." She giggled, excitedly. "Me and Livi can't wait!"

"You told Livi?" I said. I might have known she would; she and Livi have been best friends forever. They tell each other everything.

"Wasn't I supposed to?" Jordan sounded suddenly anxious. "I'm really sorry, I just did it without thinking!"

"It's OK," I said. I couldn't very well get mad at her; not after stealing her name and address. *And* her mum's name. "It doesn't matter. So long as she doesn't say anything to anyone."

Jordan eagerly assured me that she wouldn't. "I've sworn her to secrecy!"

It wasn't until the very morning of our end-of-term

show that Jordan rang me, in a state of high excitement, to say that the letter had come.

"It just plopped through the letterbox so I, like, *pounced* on it, you know? Before Mum could get there?" She giggled. "It's actually addressed to her! Do you want me to open it and tell you what it says?"

I hesitated. She was obviously dying to know! But so was I. On the other hand I didn't like the idea of Jordan getting to read *my* letter before I did. I don't get that many letters! It would be nice to be able to open it for myself. *By* myself. (Just in case it was bad news.)

"I won't look if you'd rather I didn't," said Jordan, "but don't forget it's Sunday tomorrow so even if I put it in the post right away you'd have to wait till Monday before you find out whether you've got in or not."

I curled my toes as I stood barefoot on my bedroom rug. Why couldn't they have sent the letter a day earlier? I couldn't wait till Monday! Not now I knew it was there; it would niggle at me all weekend. It might even ruin my performance. Whereas if I knew that I'd got in…

But then again, suppose I hadn't? *That* might ruin my performance!

"So what do you think?" said Jordan. "Shall I open it or not?"

I looked down at my toes, wiggling on the rug. There was a blister on one of them. I'd thought yesterday that it felt a bit sore. Dancers' toes are almost always sore; it comes from all the pointe work we do. *If I was an actress*, I thought, *it wouldn't happen*. I wouldn't have to be forever soaking my feet or bashing my shoes. *Or sewing on ribbons*. I wouldn't end up hobbling, either! Even Mum complained that she had arthritis in her toes, from all those years of dancing.

"Maddeee?" Jordan's voice bleated impatiently in my ear. "What do you want me to do?"

"OK," I said. "Open it!"

I could hear the eager ripping of the envelope even before I'd finished speaking. She couldn't wait!

I said, "*Well?*"

"I'm just getting to it! *Dear Mrs Barker, Further to*

Jordan's recent audition –" she broke off at this point to giggle – *"further to Jordan's audition we are pleased to inform you…* Oh!" Loud squeal of triumph. "How about that?" She giggled again. "They've offered me a place! I can start next term. I've just got to write and confirm – well, my mum has to write and confirm. That is –" giggle, giggle – *"someone's* mum has to write and confirm!"

I stared down again at my toes, wiggling furiously. I'd done it! I'd done it! I'd passed the audition!

"What happens now?" said Jordan.

My toes, abruptly, stopped wiggling.

"You're not going to give up the ballet?"

I actually felt quite shocked. I said, "No! Of course I'm not." One day in the future, perhaps… when I was too old to dance Juliet. But that was a long way ahead!

"It does seem a pity," said Jordan, "when they've offered you a place. I suppose you couldn't do both?"

I said, "No way!" For just a moment a mad idea flitted through my brain. I dismissed it, instantly. I'd proved what I wanted to prove! It was time to be moving on.

"I s'pose you'll have to write a letter from my mum and say you're not going to do it." Jordan sounded almost regretful. "Or –" she brightened – "you could always ring them and pretend you *are* my mum! You ought to be able to do that easily enough," she said. "I mean, considering they've offered you a place. You're obviously good. Try speaking like you're Mum and I'll tell you if you sound like her."

"I'm not going to pretend to be your mum!" I said.

"Well, you'll have to do something," said Jordan.

I said, "I know. But honestly I can't think about it right now! We've got a show tonight."

"Oh, of course, it's your end-of-term thingy, isn't it?"

I said, "Yes, it is, and I'm dancing Juliet!"

"You mean, like, Juliet from *Romeo and Juliet*? Same as the play?"

I said, "Yes."

"So who's dancing Romeo? Is it Nico?"

Liv and Jordan knew all about Nico. They knew about all the boys in my class. It was the boys that interested them rather than the ballet. They weren't really interested in ballet at all.

"*Is* it?" said Jordan.

I said, "*Yes.*"

"So…" She put on this silly slurpy voice – "he's your lover!"

"Juliet's lover," I said, rather coldly. It didn't do to encourage her. "We're doing the balcony *pas de deux*."

Jordan squealed and went, "Ooh!" And then, hopefully, "Does he look like Romeo?"

"Dunno what that means," I said.

"Well… you know! Like your brother, for instance."

"You think Sean looks like Romeo?"

"He does," said Jordan. And then she giggled again and said, "Ask Caitlyn!"

"Caitlyn's nothing to go by," I said. "She's obsessed."

"Not just her," said Jordan. "I was reading in this

article how he gets all this fanmail. Not just from this country but from all over the—"

I said, "Yeah, yeah, yeah! Like he's some kind of movie star."

"So what about Nico?"

I said, "What about him?"

"Is he like a movie star?"

"He's a *dancer*," I said.

"He could still be like a movie star!"

"Well, he's not." He was just Nico. I loved him to bits but there was nothing slurpy about it, in spite of what had happened earlier. We were partners, that was all. You're allowed to kiss your partner!

My toes had stopped wriggling and were starting to curl up.

"Look," I said, "I've got to go. Just put the letter in the post and I'll decide what to do about it later. OK?"

"OK." Jordan would obviously have liked to indulge in a long, cosy chat so that she could report back to Livi. I was sorry to disappoint her after all she'd done to help me but I do sometimes think it would make a nice change if she and Liv could take an interest in *what* I was dancing rather than who I'm dancing it with. But it was actually true that I didn't have time to waste chatting on the phone: I really did have to go.

"It's *Showtime*," I said. "I'll speak to you later!"

Chapter Ten

The end-of-term show traditionally took place in the small studio theatre at the company's regular venue, the Millennium Hall. None of us second years had ever danced there before. The third years of course had, which obviously made some of them feel rather superior. I remarked on this to Caitlyn, as we met up at Waterloo.

"I don't know what they've got to crow about… talk about big-headed!"

Caitlyn agreed. "I bet they were just as excited, first time round. Cos it is exciting, isn't it? Even you've got to be a *bit* excited!"

I said, "What do you mean, even I've got to be a bit excited?"

"Well, you're not usually! You're usually like, *been there, done that, seen it all before.*"

I frowned. I said, "Really?" Was that what people thought? Caitlyn hastened to reassure me.

"It's not your fault! It's cos you almost always *have* been there and done that and seen it all before. But you are excited today, aren't you? Please tell me that you are! Just a little bit?"

"A *little* bit?" I said. "I've never been this excited in my whole life! *Of course* I'm excited!"

How could I not be? I was dancing my dream part!

Caitlyn beamed. "It's so nice that we both feel the same way and that it's not just me for once being all stupid and naive."

Indignantly I said, "Who ever told you you were stupid?"

She pulled a face. "Tiffany."

"Oh, well, *her*. Nobody takes any notice of her! It's good to be excited," I said. "When you get that tingly feeling, just before you go on stage, when everything kind of flutters inside you, like butterflies?"

"You get that as well?" cried Caitlyn. "I thought it was just me! You always seem so cool and calm."

"I don't get stage fright," I said. "But I'm sure all the really great dancers feel a *little* bit tingly."

"Do you think your mum ever did?"

We both giggled a bit at that. It's hard to imagine Mum ever feeling tingly! Still, I think she must have done. How could you not? Even Sean – even me! Just because Dad had once accused me of being "unbearably in your face" doesn't mean I can't sometimes get tingly, the same as anyone else. I'd been in a state of total quiver before my Rosemount audition, wondering whether I was really any good or whether I was like one of Mum's pudding-faces, as she calls them, meaning pupils that can't dance being pushed by their doting parents into taking exams they haven't a chance of passing. Not that Mum ever actually puts them in for exams. She says she has her reputation to think of and tells the parents to take their precious little darlings somewhere else. But that was what had made me so quivery: the fear that I might be behaving like a precious little darling, convinced that I could act while being absolutely useless.

I wondered whether I would get quivery today. I didn't *think* that I would. A bit tingly, perhaps, cos it was after all an important occasion. But not actually quivery. Tingly was excitement: quivery was lack of confidence. How could I lack confidence when I had Nico to depend on? We'd been rehearsing right up until the last moment and I trusted him completely. I couldn't have asked for a better partner!

Curtain was due up at two o'clock. As humble second years we were on first, leaving pride of place – in other words, the second half – to our elders and betters, otherwise known as Year Three. Some of the third years could be quite snooty. One of them, as they sailed past us through the stage door, actually dared to pat Tiffany on the head. Tiffany, of all people!

"Don't worry, little one! Your turn will come."

I felt for her, though in truth she'd totally brought it on herself. Just a few seconds before she'd been complaining, in her loud clanging voice, how it was so not fair, letting people hog the whole of the second half just because they happened to be a year ahead of us. Now she was all red and spluttering.

"Patronising cow!"

"Look who's talking," muttered Roz.

It has to be said, nobody can be more patronising than our Tiffany. She'll be positively unbearable by the time we're in our third year! She was already being quite tiresome enough, preening herself over the running order for the first half of the show, which Mrs Elkins had recently posted. Tiffany was to open with her *ZigZag* variation, followed by Mei and Christopher in *Lovers' Meeting*. Nico and I, with our balcony scene, were at the end, with just the mad romp of *Bombe Surprise* to round everything off. Tiffany had already worked out, to her own satisfaction, that if she couldn't actually close the show then being first on was the next best thing, if not indeed actually *the* best.

"*Bombe*," she loftily informed us, "is just a lollipop… just a bit of nonsense to bring the curtain down. You wouldn't want to open with it. You need something quality to set the tone. And speaking personally," she added, in case anyone was interested, which they weren't, "I definitely wouldn't want to be followed by it. Talk about from the sublime to the ridiculous! A total mood breaker."

Nobody argued with her: nobody could be bothered. We had more important things to worry about than Tiffany and her insane desire to puff herself up. I really couldn't waste my energy on her rantings and ravings. Sitting before the mirror, seeing to my make-up, I did my best to blot out not just Tiffany but all the rest of the usual dressing-room frenzy. People pathetically bleating about their hair or their shoes or their costumes.

Hair that wouldn't go right, shoes that weren't comfortable, costumes coming apart at the seams. Tragedy and disaster in every corner of the room! Normally I'd have joined in, just to be companionable; today it was a distraction. Not being grand or anything, but all I wanted to do was find a quiet place inside my head where I could hide myself away and prepare.

Promptly at two o'clock the curtain went up. I went to stand in the wings, watching Tiffany being impressively acrobatic in her *ZigZag* variation. She was good, and she knew it. She flashed me a look of triumph as she made her exit. Slowly I turned away, intending to go back to the dressing room to put the finishing touches to my hair and make-up, but as I walked along the passage the door to the boys' dressing room opened and Oliver came out. I could see, even from a distance, that something was wrong. He seemed unsteady on his feet. I watched in horror as he took a couple of uncertain steps before very slowly collapsing to the ground, sliding down with his back against the wall.

"Olly!" I raced towards him. As I did so, the dressing-room door opened and Nico appeared, looking worried. He said afterwards he had thought earlier that Oliver didn't look too well. Together we crouched by his side.

"What is it?" I said. "What's wrong? Nico, get Mrs Elkins! Quickly!"

Nico shot off.

"Olly?" I said. "Are you OK?"

Oliver gave me a faint apologetic grin. "I think I've got chicken pox," he said.

I said, "*What?*"

"Chicken pox… you'd better not come too close."

"That's all right," I said. "I've had it." I didn't *think* you could get it twice; but even if you could I wasn't about to leave him there. "You look terrible!" I said. "You're all sweating. You've obviously got a temperature."

"And spots." He groaned. "They were there when I woke up. My landlady's kids have all got it. I was hoping I'd be OK. But it's all right, I can still dance!"

He plainly couldn't. He just about managed to struggle

to his feet as Nico came racing back with Mrs Elkins, but promptly sank down again, defeated.

"He's got chicken pox," I said.

"Yes, I can see," said Mrs Elkins. "Oh dear, Oliver! You do look in a bad way."

"I can still dance!"

He struggled again to get up, but very gently Mrs Elkins pushed him back down.

"Not in that state, you can't. Maddy, you'd better run and tell Caitlyn we're going to have to pull her performance. It's sad, but there's no one else who knows the part. It's not your fault, Oliver! It's just one of those things. Maddy, go! What are you waiting for?"

Breathlessly I said, "There is someone who knows the part!"

"Who?"

"Sean," I said. "He's out there! In the audience. I'll go and get him!"

"Maddy, no!" Mrs Elkins grabbed at my arm. "You

can't ask a senior member of the company to fill in for a second year, even if he is your brother."

"Oh, please," I begged, "please! He won't mind. He'll be only too happy!"

To be honest I wasn't so sure about him being happy, but how could he possibly refuse? It would break Caitlyn's heart if she couldn't go on!

"Please let me," I said.

"Well…" I could see that Mrs Elkins was wavering. "Well, all right, you can give it a go. But don't badger him!"

"I won't," I promised. And to Nico I added, "Don't say anything to Caitlyn. She'll die of nerves if she knows who's going to be dancing with her!"

"Well, you'd better get a move on," said Nico. "If he's going to find time to change—"

"He'll need the costume," I said. "Go up to Wardrobe, they should have it there!"

"OK."

Nico seemed a bit bewildered by me taking charge,

but someone had to! Mrs Elkins had enough to do seeing to poor Olly.

I slipped through the pass door and crept on tiptoe into the auditorium. Needless to say, we are not supposed to go into the auditorium in full costume and make-up when a show is in progress. Fortunately I'd peeked through the curtains earlier on and knew where Sean was sitting: with Danny, and Mum and Dad, at the end of the first row. It would have been truly embarrassing if I'd had to go roaming the aisles in search of him. Even as it was I was in full view of Ms Hickman, sitting just a bit further along. I could almost see her eyebrows doing that thing that they did, shooting up into her hairline like a pair of angry question marks, her eyes homing in on me like lasers. But I didn't have time to worry about Ms Hickman. I slithered up to Sean, urgently crouching by his side.

"Quick! Come! We need you!"

He whispered, "What?"

"We need you! Now!"

I tugged at him, and in some bewilderment he allowed me to drag him off, back through the pass door.

"Mads?" He waited till we were safely out of sight of Ms Hickman and her shooting eyebrows. "What am I doing here?"

"It's Olly," I said. "He's got the chicken pox, he can't dance, and you're the only one who knows the part. It's for Caitlyn," I pleaded. "It means so much to her! She'll be broken-hearted if we have to cancel. I've already sent Nico up to Wardrobe for your costume... *please*, Sean! Please say you'll do it!"

I thought for a moment he was going to tell me not to be so ridiculous, how could he go on at this late stage? But then he said, "It's *Spectre*, right?"

"Right!" I nodded. "She's on in five minutes and she doesn't know about Olly cos I thought if I t—"

"OK. Don't panic. We'll see what we can do."

Nico had already appeared, sprinting triumphantly towards us with Sean's *Spectre* costume slung over his shoulder. Sean wasted no time, simply snatched it and ran. Nico said, "Phew!" And then, "Has anyone told Caitlyn yet?"

I shook my head. "Not yet."

"Don't you think we ought?"

"No time," I said. "It would frighten the life out of her."

Nico pulled a face. He obviously thought someone should have warned her. Maybe they should; I just hadn't wanted to alarm her so close to the performance. Surely it was better that she woke from her dream to a genuine surprise rather than working herself up into a state of total panic? Whatever, it was too late to do anything about it now.

Nico and I stood together in the wings, watching as Caitlyn ran on stage and sank down into her chair in the moonlight, to close her eyes and dream of the handsome young man she had just met at the ball.

I whispered fiercely to Nico, "Where is he?"

"He's on his way. Don't worry!"

It was nerve-racking, to say the least. If Sean hadn't arrived by the time Caitlyn opened her eyes...

I tightened my fingers round Nico's wrist. "You were right! I should have warned her!"

Nico shook his head. "She'll be OK."

But would she? She'd never danced with Sean before; she was in total awe of him. Suppose she just went to pieces? And it would be all my fault! I should have got word to her. At least that way she'd have been a bit prepared. As it was —

Right on cue, Sean made his entrance.

"Told you," said Nico. "She'll be fine."

I became suddenly aware that Mrs Elkins had joined us. She, too, was watching the stage intently. Caitlyn opened her eyes, and we all of us held our breath. And then Sean slowly extended his hand and Caitlyn, as if still in a dream, obediently took it and allowed him to lead her down stage.

That was the moment that I knew for sure it was going to be all right. For all that he is so good at swashbuckling roles such as Mercutio, Sean is actually a very considerate partner. He would be kind to Caitlyn. She would be safe in his hands.

I let out my breath in a great *whoosh*. Mrs Elkins smiled at me.

"Well done, Maddy! You saved the day."

"And I didn't badger him," I said. Just in case Ms Hickman should come raging after me demanding to know what right I had to ask a leading member of the company to stand in for a lowly second year.

"Don't worry." Mrs Elkins said it soothingly. "You did the right thing. And between you and me –" she lowered her voice, conspiratorially – "I don't think your brother is the sort to allow himself to be badgered!"

The curtain came down to tumultuous applause. Sean and Caitlyn left the stage, Caitlyn obviously still in a world of her own, scarcely even aware of me and Nico standing there. Sean winked at me and whispered, "Go for it, girl!" Nico gave my hand a comforting squeeze.

"Showtime!"

There was no time to quiver. I quickly ran on stage and took my position on the balcony, leaning forward, eyes eagerly searching in the moonlight for any sign that Romeo might have come. And then he was there, at the foot of the balcony, and I was rushing down the steps to take his hand. We'd only had one rehearsal with the balcony in place and I'd had a few nightmares about the steps. What if I slipped? Or tripped? Or fell? It would ruin the whole performance! But of course I didn't, and even if I had Nico would have caught me. He knew I'd been a bit nervous about the steps. As he took my hand and we moved to the centre of the stage he whispered, "Made it!"

It was at that moment that a most extraordinary sensation came over me. One I'd never had before. Almost what I think is called *out of body*. I no longer felt like me, dancing with Nico, but Juliet dancing with Romeo. For those few precious moments on stage I felt that I actually *was* Juliet. No longer acting: *being*. It was like I didn't have to listen to the music, or count the beats, or remember my steps: they were all a part of me. Part of Juliet. I could have danced on forever!

Exhilaration was still bubbling up inside me even after we'd taken our bow and were leaving the stage.

"Did you feel it?" I said to Nico. "Did you feel what I felt?"

He nodded, solemnly. "It was awesome," he said.

"I've never felt like that before!"

"Me neither."

"It was like we really *were* I—"

I was about to say *lovers*, but stopped myself just in time. Nico, with a grin, said it for me.

"Lovers?"

I nodded, breathlessly. My cheeks were burning up again. What was happening to me? I was getting as bad as Caitlyn!

"One of these days —" Nico said it very solemnly — "we'll do the whole ballet."

"Is that a promise?" I said.

He squeezed my hand. "You'd better believe it!"

I did. With all my heart!

Back in the dressing room, removing my make-up, putting on my ordinary street clothes, I began very slowly to come back to earth. We'd arranged, afterwards – Mum and Dad, Sean and Danny, me and Caitlyn, even Caitlyn's mum – to go out for a special tea at a posh hotel in the West End. Jen couldn't join us as she wanted to get back for Thomas, but with a bit of help from me, Caitlyn had managed to get her mum to say she would come.

"I'm so glad," I said, as we finished changing and made our way to the stage door. "It wouldn't feel right without her." Caitlyn had been doubtful, at first, whether even I would be able to talk her round. Me and my powers of persuasion! But Caitlyn's mum is a very shy and quiet sort of person. "If she's scared of Mum and Dad," I said – I know that lots of people are – "she can always talk to Sean and Danny." They're not in the least bit scary.

"It's not that she's scared," said Caitlyn. "She's just not used to mixing with celebs."

"What's she going to do when you're one?" I said. "And don't try telling me you won't be, cos after that performance I bet Madam's already got your career mapped out!"

Caitlyn's cheeks flushed a happy pink. "I couldn't have done it without Sean."

"Well, no, if he hadn't been there," I agreed. "Poor old Olly couldn't even walk in a straight line!"

We fell silent a moment, thinking of Oliver. We both felt badly for him.

"Oh, but you should have seen your face!" I said. "When you opened your eyes and saw who it was on stage with you!"

"I know, I couldn't believe it! I thought I really *was* dreaming."

"I bet some people in the audience thought they were dreaming! There wasn't any time to make an announcement. We didn't even have time to tell *you*."

"Probably just as well," said Caitlyn. "I'd have been terrified!"

I shook my head. "I don't know how anyone can be terrified of Sean. He's really quite nice – and he's a very generous partner."

"It's not that." Caitlyn's cheeks had turned from happy pink to a deep, blushing crimson. "Do you remember, ages and ages ago, I told you about this dream I had, and you asked if it was to do with ballet, and I said yes, and you said was it a particular part I wanted to dance or was it a particular person I wanted to dance with, and—"

"And you got all embarrassed and wouldn't say!"

"So then you made me promise that if ever it came true I'd tell you—"

"And now it has! But it wasn't any secret," I said. "I always knew that was your dream, to dance with Sean. I just hope it lived up to expectations."

"I didn't have any expectations," said Caitlyn. "Even now I can't quite believe it!"

Her eyes were shining – and so was her face. With cold cream! She'd obviously been too excited to remove her make-up properly.

"Did you know you've still got great splodges of cream all over you?" I said.

"No!" She smeared at her cheek. "Where?"

"All over. Hang on!" I dug my hand in my coat pocket for a tissue. As I fished for one, something slipped out and fluttered to the floor. I knew at once what it was: it was the sheet of paper Mrs Ashworth had given me with my audition details on it. After I'd had the audition I'd obviously stuffed it in my pocket and forgotten all about it. I quickly bent to snatch it up before Caitlyn could see the name **ROSEMOUNT** written in bold letters across the top. But too late!

"What was that?" she said, as I hastily shoved it back in my pocket.

"Just a bit of paper," I said.

"Did it say **ROSEMOUNT** on it?"

"No! Well – yes. Maybe. But it's nothing important! It's all over and done with. It was just something I thought I might be interested in but it totally wasn't possible and anyway it doesn't matter any more cos

I've finally made up my mind that all I want to do is dance!"

Caitlyn was looking puzzled. "What are you talking about? I don't understand! Didn't you already want to dance?"

It was hard to explain. I did my best. There was a difference, I told her, between accepting that you were going to do something because that's how it had always been, ever since you could remember, and suddenly realising that it was what you really passionately *did* want to do. The *only* thing you wanted to do. To be the very best dancer you possibly could!

"And what's more," I said, "I'm going to do it as *me*. Not as Mum and Dad's daughter, or Sean O'Brien's sister, but *me* in my own right!"

Caitlyn gave a little laugh. I stared at her, hurt. What was so funny?

"Sorry!" She straightened her face, trying to look serious.

I said, "*What?*"

"You in your own right..." The giggles had burst through again. "Like you could ever be anything else!"

"Well..." I gave a reluctant grin. Maybe she had a point. Looking back, I seemed to have spent the whole of the last two years proving to myself that I was me. Just me, in my own right. Maybe none of it had really been necessary.

I slipped my arm through Caitlyn's.

"Come on," I said. "Let's go and celebrate!"

If you loved *STAR QUALITY* and *SHOWTIME*, don't forget to read about Maddy and caitlyn in *BORN TO DANCE*

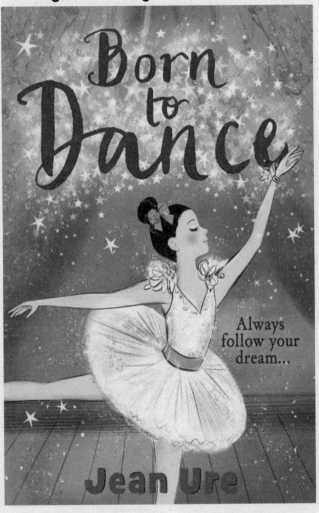

Don't miss Maddy's second dance
adventure in *STAR QUALITY*

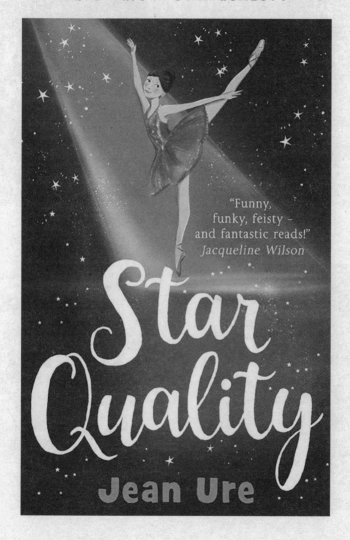

More from Jean Ure...

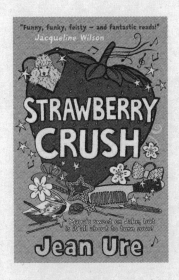

"Funny, funky, feisty – and fantastic reads!"
Jacqueline Wilson

SECRET MEETING

Jean Ure

"Funny, funky, feisty – and fantastic reads!"
Jacqueline Wilson

LEMONADE SKY

Jean Ure

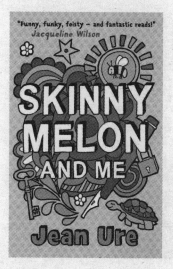

"Funny, funky, feisty – and fantastic reads!"
Jacqueline Wilson

SKINNY MELON AND ME

Jean Ure

"Funny, funky, feisty – and fantastic reads!"
Jacqueline Wilson

PUMPKIN PIE

Jean Ure

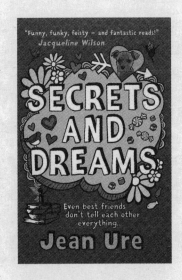

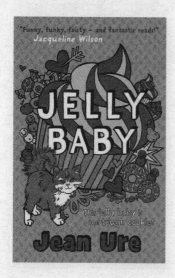

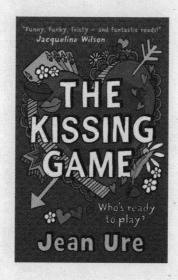

And for fans of FRANKIE FOSTER...

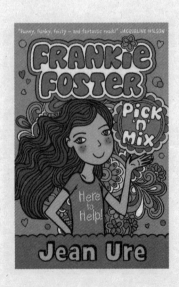